Her arms cradling a multihued bouquet, Kathleen started down a grassy embankment skirting the parking lot. She took two strides and froze. Her head lifted. She stared at the grounded shuttle before her. The blossoms tumbled from her arms as her right hand dropped to the .45 strapped to her hip.

"Noooo!"

Walker's scream drowned in the sizzling hiss of eleven rifles. Bolts of intense blue sliced through the night as burning pearls of light shot out at Kathleen.

One . . . two . . . five . . . ten . . . He lost count of the flaring globes of death that struck her vulnerable body. Like a mannequin with a madman yanking at its strings, she jerked and twisted under the impacts, spinning about with arms flying wildly before she crumpled face-down in the grass.

How? Walker's mind railed. The toxin, V-Dust—Janus said the Visitors had been driven away, had returned to their own world! How could a shuttle be here? *How?*

THE CHICAGO CONVERSION

Geo. W. Proctor

PINNACLE BOOKS      **NEW YORK**

This novel is a work of fiction. Names, characters, places, and incidents are either the product of the author's imagination or are used fictitiously. Any resemblance to actual events or places or persons, living or dead, is entirely coincidental.

V: THE CHICAGO CONVERSION

Copyright © 1985 by Warner Bros., Inc.

An original Pinnacle Books edition, published for the first time anywhere.

First printing/January 1985

ISBN: 0-523-42429-9

Can. ISBN: 0-523-43417-0

Cover photo/art used with permission from Lick Observatory.

Printed in the United States of America

PINNACLE BOOKS, INC.
1430 Broadway
New York, New York 10018

9   8   7   6   5   4   3   2   1

This one is for:

JEANNE CLANAN
BRENT HAMPTON
RUTH HAMPTON
BECKY MATTHEWS
STEVE OLLER
TERESA PATTERSON
BOB WAYNE

without whose help this would have never been.

Chapter One

Death leaped toward the Chicago sky in a profusion of color. Thousands upon thousands of children's balloons danced upward on a gentle morning breeze. For those below with necks craned to stare at the cloudless blue, the multihued array rivaled the festive displays of a hundred sporting events where humankind often offered such airborne garlands to the fleeting glory of its athletic demigods.

Balloons—red, yellow, orange, blue, green, purple, pink—helium-filled balloons meant to be tied on a string for a Sunday afternoon stroll in the park bobbed, wove, and soared into the face of a summer morning. Never had death been celebrated in such joyous, merry splendor.

In spite of the colorful sea of wind-bounced balloons, celebration was far from Chicagoans' minds. The balloons formed a front-line offensive as humanity waged war—global war—for its right to remain on the planet that had given it birth!

The plump, elastic belly of each rubbery bubble lay laden with death, a common kitchen tablespoon of shifting, rust-hued powder. V-Dust, Lizard Arsenic, V-Con, Snake Powder were but a few of the names resistance fighters across the world had jokingly dubbed the substance while they prepared for this the final battle.

Now there were no jokes.

In deadly earnest they unleashed the virulent bacterial toxin upon the alien life form that had come to dominate Earth—a life form that had traveled 8.7 light-years across the yawning chasm of space in gargantuan ships equaling the size of a modern metropolis. From the fourth planet of the star Sirius they came, calling themselves the Visitors. With open hands they promised friendship, and with gentle smiles and soft words they offered to share their vast wealth of knowledge.

Humanity had greeted them in peace, allowing the alien travelers open access to every small niche of human existence. The Visitors insinuated themselves into those niches, subtly, allowing their hosts time to accept their constant presence as they wove themselves deeper and deeper into every stratum of the human social structure.

Quiet Visitor influence here and there went unnoticed, paving the way for ever greater flexing of alien muscle. Before a dazed human population knew how or why, the Visitors, with their endless units of shock troopers, had supplanted human authority. They controlled transportation, communications, law enforcement, and local and national governments. The open hand of friendship had been transformed into an iron fist of suppression!

The human spirit did not die. Men, women, and children banded together in a global underground network of resistance fighters. Through their efforts and sacrifices, the Visitors were unmasked. The fleshlike, human makeup they wore was ripped away to unveil reptilian faces of green mottled with black.

More horrible was the purpose of the Visitors' journey from distant Sirius—they intended to suck Earth dry!

The abundant waters washing over humanity's home world were a prize of immeasurable wealth to the Visitors whose own planet's landmasses dwarfed its tiny seas and the ribbonlike trickles the Visitors called rivers. Earth offered another abundant natural resource for the extraterrestrial invaders—humankind itself. For another shortage—of food—existed on the Visitors' home planet.

The majority of humanity complacently accepted Visitor domination. Gullibly they swallowed the lies the aliens spoon-fed them over their living room television sets. How easy it was to believe the lies rather than examine rumors that populations of whole cities and towns had vanished overnight, packed away like sides of beef in the Visitors' great Mother Ships. And who could truly believe that human governmental officials had somehow been brainwashed, their personalities remolded, converted until they were no more than zombies designed to carry out Visitor bidding?

No one except the ever-expanding resistance movement. They had *seen*, and they *knew*. A pocket of fighters in Los Angeles, many of them scientists escaping the Visitors' regime, developed a bacterial toxin capable of killing the reptilian Visitors within two minutes after it was introduced into the aliens' respiratory system. At the same time, the deadly agent left terrestrial life forms unharmed. Both the toxin and an antitoxin to protect fifth columnists within the Visitors' own numbers were secreted along underground railroads throughout the world.

It was this poison that rose to the sky above Chicago in a flood of helium-filled balloons today. The same toxin that a small armada of private airplanes and hot-air balloons showered into the atmosphere in bloody contrails streaming behind their small crafts. On the ground, armed with grenades packed with V-Dust and sandblasting equipment to spray the toxin, an army of resistance fighters swept over

Michigan Avenue and Adams Street to storm the Art
Institute of Chicago where Visitor security forces were
headquartered.

Even as human and alien fell beneath the blasts of armor-
piercing bullets or the blue pulse beams of energy weapons
in Chicago's heart, the country surrounding the great
metropolis erupted in a brilliant burst of color. A second
wave of toxin-laden balloons danced into the sky.

Jeff Stevenson balanced precariously amid the upper
limbs of an ancient cherry tree in Lake Zurich, forty miles
northwest of Chicago's Loop. He hefted a pair of army
surplus field binoculars and peered toward the city.

"Can you see anything, Jeff?" his wife, Linda, called
from the ground below.

A smile lit Jeff's deeply suntanned face while he watched
a distant black spot maneuver beneath the nose of the
monstrous Mother Ship hanging over Chicago. The dark
dot, no larger than a gnat through the binoculars, left a
broad trail behind it in the air. Like the smoky contrail of a
skywriter, it spewed V-Dust in the form of a single letter, a
gigantic red V—the international calling card of the
resistance. V for Victory!

Jeff's mouth hardened. A blue bolt of sizzling light shot
from the saucer-shaped end of the Visitor craft. The gnatlike
dot vanished. Yanking the field glasses from his eyes, he
slammed them back into a case slung at his waist.

That was only one of us, he reassured himself. *The V
remains. That's what's important—the V remains!*

"Jeff?" Linda called out again. "What can you see?"

Jeff Stevenson smiled down at the petite redhead staring
up from below as he began to scramble toward the ground.
"The Mother Ship . . ."

"And the balloons? Can't you see them?" Linda frowned when he dropped to the ground.

"Like flies swarming up from the city." Jeff's grin widened. "It's unbelievable! I've never seen anything like it!"

Linda's right hand dropped to her slim waist. Steel hissed against leather. The long steel tooth of a silvery hunting knife slipped free of a sheath hung from her belt. "Let's add a few more flies to the ointment!"

With a wink, she pivoted and ran toward an open field stretching north of the tree. Jeff slid a similar blade from a scabbard dangling behind a holstered .45-caliber automatic perched on his right hip. Gaze lifting to his wife, he trotted after the slender redhead.

Through waist-high weeds covering a field once used to grow sweet corn, they moved. The husband and wife stopped when they reached a lumpy, shifting mound at the center of the clearing. This close to it the camouflaged tarpaulin appeared blatantly obvious, Jeff thought. But, then, the tarp was never meant to deceive ground troops but to conceal the deadly cache beneath from the occasional Visitor squad vehicles that flew reconnaissance over deserted Lake Zurich.

Linda's head turned to Jeff, her emerald eyes agleam. He nodded. Without hesitation the two bent. The honed edges of their hunting knives slashed two of the staked cords that held the tarpaulin to the ground. The canvas quivered as though something beneath it—something alive—were straining to be free of the confining weight.

Again the man's and woman's blades lashed out, and again. At an equal pace, they worked around the edges of the tarp, slicing each cord solidly staked into the fertile earth. They halted when only the last side of the canvas remained secured to the ground. Standing straight, Jeff and

Linda Stevenson smiled at each other while they resheathed their blades.

"Time to set those flies loose!" Jeff tilted his head toward the opposite end of the tarpaulin.

Linda's smile widened and she nodded in reply before stepping to the open end of the canvas and grasping a corner. Jeff reached down and took the opposite corner. Together they wrenched the tarp back. A thousand brightly colored balloons leaped toward the cloudless sky, each bearing another tablespoon of red toxin into the air.

"There it is." Linda's voice came soft and solemn when she stepped to her husband's side and pointed to a Day-Glored orb adorned with the smiling face of Mickey Mouse.

Jeff found his wife's hand and squeezed it. Mickey was special; he was for Carla. The Walt Disney creation had been Carla's favorite cartoon character.

Jeff closed his eyes to stem the welling tears and to blot out the memories of a night six months ago. He and Linda had left their four-year-old daughter with a babysitter and driven into nearby Barrington to catch the latest Steven Spielberg flick. Goosepimply from the director's newest collection of special-effects crawlies and beasties, they had shared a double scoop of daiquiri ice at Baskin-Robbins, then had driven back to Lake Zurich.

Only, there was no Lake Zurich, just empty houses and buildings. They found a dying policeman, collapsed among garbage containers in an alley, his chest seared by a blast from a Visitor energy rifle, and from him they learned of the horror that had transpired in their few hours of absence.

A fleet of Visitor shuttles had dropped out of the night sky. From each swarmed an army of shock troopers in their red uniforms, black boots, and helmets. In a matter of two hours every home and building in Lake Zurich was emptied. The population of a whole town was herded like cattle into the waiting shuttles. When the craft vanished into the night, so had four-year-old Carla Stevenson.

Jeff shook his head and opened his eyes, staring at the cloud of soaring balloons. A resistance reconnaissance team who entered Lake Zurich the next morning revealed the gruesome purpose of the Visitors' raid. Since then Linda and he had only thought of their young daughter in the past tense. Though she might still be alive aboard one of the monstrous Mother Ships—they had heard rumors that a similar thing had happened to the son of the Visitor-hunted newsman Michael Donovan—they could not live on false hope, on a dream that might never be.

Instead they fought. At the side of others who realized the fate of humanity was at stake, Jeff and Linda Stevenson had helped the Chicago area resistance movement establish a headquarters in a deserted hotel along the shores of the small lake from which the town took its name. They did so that other four-year-old children might live. And they waited until they could avenge the daughter who had been taken from them.

Today Mickey will make the snakes pay! Jeff thought while the unleashed balloons floated higher.

The internal pressure of each colorful orb had been carefully calculated so it would explode within a specific portion of the atmosphere. There the virulent bacteria released would multiply. With each gentle rain, each booming thunderstorm, it would fall to the earth, contaminating the water, becoming part of each living organism, weaving itself into every tiny niche of Earth's food chain, making the whole planet poisonous to the human-disguised reptiles who sought to suck it dry!

For Carla! Jeff silently cheered as he squeezed his wife's hand again. "We'd better head back to headquarters. Things will be poppin' soon."

A pained grimace played across Linda's lips in reaction to

her husband's unintentional pun. She leaned forward and tenderly kissed his mouth. It was a kiss, Jeff realized, that was as much for Carla as for him.

"Have I told you how much I love you?" he asked. She shook her head and he smiled. "Remind me to do so when we have more time."

Linda's right arm rose; her fist balled. Before she could deliver a playful punch to his arm, she froze. Her eyes went wide. A piteous whimper escaped her lips.

Jeff's head jerked around. Five Visitor squad vehicles silently darted from the sky in delta formation. The tip of that tight V dipped toward the field.

"Run!" Jeff shoved Linda toward the cherry tree while he yanked the .45 from its holster. "Take cover!"

Her questioning look lasted just a split second before she pivoted and darted for the relative security of the cherry tree's leafy boughs. Her legs carried her but two bounding strides before blinding blue bolts of pulse-beam energy erupted from the triangular nose of the lead craft.

Linda's scream rent the morning silence as the first sizzling blast ripped between her shoulder blades, ending her life.

"No!" Agony tore from Jeff's chest and throat. Linda's lifeless body collapsed, swallowed by the jungle of weeds covering the field. *"Nooooo!"*

First Carla—now Linda! His sanity frayed, then snapped. The lizards, the damned lizards, had taken all from him, robbed him of his reasons for living.

Both hands about the .45, he swirled and jerked the automatic high. Stiff-armed, he held it into the faces of the approaching Visitor shuttles. He curled a finger around the trigger and squeezed.

Glaring, globelike balls of blue energy crackled from the noses of all five ships. Before a single shot barked from the pistol, Jeff Stevenson died, his living flesh instantly transformed to smoldering charcoal.

"An unexpected but useful check of the squad's weaponry, don't you think, Captain?" Gerald's words reverberated with a sibilant hiss as he forced his forked reptilian tongue to accommodate the alien syllables of English.

"A waste of a fine feast," the shock trooper captain answered with a wistful shake of his head. He turned a helmeted head from the dead man and woman below and glanced at his blonde, blue-eyed human-disguised companion in the squad vehicle's pilot's couch.

"But a waste of which Our Great Leader would approve, Frank." Gerald eased back the controls. The craft leveled and nosed toward a sun-glinting lake that lay directly ahead. Gerald tapped a yellow button on the left arm of the control couch. Intership communications opened. "One minute to touchdown. Prepare your troops for evacuation and immediate engagement of the enemy."

"Our Leader will approve of every death that comes this morning, as will Commander Alicia," Frank agreed. "Nor will your part in breaking the back of this bothersome human resistance go unnoticed." Frank's approving smile vanished beneath the gas mask he fitted over mouth and nostrils. His face then disappeared when he lowered the dark smoked faceplate to his helmet.

With cool restraint, Gerald repressed the smile that sought to lift the corners of his human-shaped lips. When he had volunteered to infiltrate the fifth columnists within Alicia's Chicago Mother Ship four months ago, he had been a lowly lieutenant, a faceless soldier among the thousands aboard the huge vessel. His exposure of twenty-five traitors within the Mother Ship's hull two weeks after he undertook the assignment brought the first promotion.

Since then he had soared to the rank of high captain—a notch above Frank, who had been his superior a few short months ago. His work among the fifth columnists aiding the human resistance had first caught Commander Alicia's eye. After all, he was the one that first brought her word of the "secret weapon" the humans intended to unleash this morning.

In a few minutes his military prowess would draw the attention of the invasion's supreme commander, John. With the 250 shock troopers he commanded, Gerald would annihilate the Chicago resistance force and their headquarters before they had the opportunity to employ their secret weapon.

With such a victory, who knows what rewards will come my way. A hint of a smile touched his lips. *Military commander? Captain of Alicia's personal security force?* The last prospect was particularly intriguing, since Alicia shared her bed with the present commander of security.

"Any report on the purpose of these balloons yet?" The muffled reverberation of Frank's voice shattered Gerald's bedroom fantasies.

"Nothing solid." Across the lake Gerald saw the white form of the abandoned hotel in which the resistance fighters hid. "Command believes they are an ineffectual attempt at confusion, or perhaps a signal of some sort."

Silently the squad vessel and its sister ships shot over the small lake. Gerald hovered in midair a moment, then eased forward on the controls. The craft and its four companions drifted down to settle in an empty parking lot behind the hotel.

"Red unit, hit the main structure." Gerald gave the final instruction as he thumbed the yellow button on the couch's arm to life again. "Blue unit, concentrate on the ten cottages along the lake's shore. Resistance communications are housed in the fifth cottage. I want that knocked out as soon as possible!"

With that, Gerald flipped a switch opening the doors to the belly of the shuttle. The scramble of booted feet came from behind him when he turned and nodded to Frank. Together they shoved from their couches and followed the fifty armored and helmeted shock troopers who darted into the hotel parking area.

Outside red-uniformed troops poured from the five shuttles. In precise formation the rifle-clutching soldiers divided into two units, one running for the hotel's main building, the other swinging toward the white cottages along the lake.

"Not even a guard posted," Frank said as his helmeted head turned to Gerald. "I think we caught them napping. They haven't woken up yet!"

Not we—me! Gerald already tasted the sweetness of Alicia's lips, the coolness of her body against his scales— her real body, unencumbered by an awkward human disguise. *I never thought it would be this easy!* His gaze surveyed the peaceful scene around him. *Never this easy.*

"High Captain," a voice crackled from the earphone plugged into Gerald's left ear, "Red leader here. First floor secure with no resistance met."

"No resistance?" Gerald's eyes widened beneath the near-black lenses of the sunglasses he wore. "That can't be! The hotel was packed yesterday. Over three hundred humans . . ."

"Blue leader reports the first two cottages are empty." Frank's voice cut off his companion.

"Empty?" Deep furrows ran across Gerald's brow. "How can that—" He caught himself. Drawing a deep breath, he repressed the panic that threatened to dissolve his composure. "Frank, I want to examine those cottages myself."

Even as they walked through the quiet morning toward the lake, the earphone buzzed again with the Red leader's report that all floors of the hotel were secured—and all were empty! Gerald gnashed the double row of reptilian teeth hidden behind his human mask. Something had caused the humans to flee their headquarters. But what?

Damn! What did I overlook? What did I miss? Calmly he replayed in his mind everything he had learned of today's attack and the resistance's secret weapon. *Nothing! I overlooked nothing!*

The bark of explosive projectile weapons rent the morning's stillness as Gerald and Frank approached the first of the cottages. The sizzle of energy bolts from the muzzles of the shock trooper rifles sounded in immediate reply.

Gerald pivoted to see four of his soldiers crumple to the ground. Blossoms of orange and red fire came from the windows of the fifth white cottage—the small house containing resistance communications. Another round of fire cracked from the open windows of the small building. Three more soldiers fell, and the remaining troops started to scatter, seeking cover.

"*No!*" Gerald's voice screamed out above the din of battle. "Take the house! Advance! Advance! Take them! Open fire!"

One hundred and seventeen black rifles swung about to home in on the white house. Blue bursts of pulsing light spat from their muzzles; a spray of energy converged on the open windows. Human cries resounded from within.

Twice more the reports of gunpowder weapons barked to bring an eighth shock trooper to his knees. Again the electric sizzle of the energy rifles answered.

Gerald heard a cry from the house, then nothing. He held up an arm. The bombarding bolts halted. His head cocking from side to side, the high captain listened and heard nothing. His arm fell.

The shock troopers advanced with Gerald and Frank behind them. Reaching the cottage, five of the forward men ran to the door, blasted it open, then ducked inside. A minute later one appeared in the doorway, waving an all clear.

"Blue leader," Gerald ordered when he and Frank moved toward the secured house, "continue your search of the remaining cottages."

Gerald's gaze moved over the interior of the cottage. The three small rooms revealed the sprawled bodies of eight men and women who had died in the senseless defense of the house. *Fools! What did they hope to gain? Surely they realized they were outnumbered.*

"Our fire knocked out their radio." Frank's helmeted head tilted to a smoldering mass of melted metal in the corner of the living room. The heap of slag was all that remained of the radio and the portable generator used to power it. "I doubt if they had the time to warn anyone of the attack."

Gerald nodded although doubt and anger railed through his brain. *Attack? What attack? Where are the human fighters? Eight is not the more than three hundred who cowered here yesterday. . . . Where is the victory in cutting down a mere eight?*

"High Captain, I think you'd better take a look at what we've found in the last cottage," the voice of the Blue unit leader cracked from the earphone.

Without reply, Gerald motioned Frank from the house, then strode down the small line of cottages. The Blue leader and three of his men dragged two cardboard boxes out the door of the last house.

"What is so important, Sergeant?" Gerald demanded when he reached the men.

"I'm not certain." The soldier shook his helmeted head. "First I found these."

Gerald accepted two plastic bags the sergeant handed him. Each was packed with white pills twice the size of the aspirin tablets humans were so fond of as a remedy for their myriad of aches and pains. Gerald flipped the bags over. A white adhesive label clung near the closed mouth of each. Scrawled on the tags were the words "ANTITOXIN: 100 COUNT."

"Any idea what they are?" Frank asked, staring at the bags.

Gerald frowned and shook his head, then glanced back at the sergeant. "What else did you feel was so important for me to see?"

"These." He pointed to the two boxes the men tilted forward. "The cottage is packed with this."

Gerald's frown deepened. The two boxes were stuffed with plastic packets of red powder that from all appearances looked like dried human blood. The labels on these simply read "V-DUST."

"Strange," Frank mused when he lifted one of the bags. "Ever seen this before?"

Gerald shook his head. He didn't have time to be bothered with an examination of the resistance fighters' supplies. Where were the humans who had filled the hotel yesterday? And where was their secret weapon?

"Wonder what it is? Food concentrate?" Frank ran a gloved finger into the bag's mouth, opening it. The same finger dipped into the powder. It clung to his leather glove when he withdrew his finger.

While Gerald ordered his troops to regroup at the squad vehicles, Frank edged back his faceplate and pulled the gas mask from his face. He sniffed at the red powder and moved his head from side to side.

"Doesn't have an appetizing odor." A long, red, forked tongue flicked from his human-masked mouth and lapped at the rust-colored powder. "It tastes even worse. I don't see how even humans could eat this garbage! But, then, I don't see why we should worry what hu—uh—arrragh!"

Gerald's head jerked around when the captain choked. The bag dropped from Frank's palm and spilled to the ground as both his hands snaked to the neck of his uniform, ripping it open.

"Can't bre— Can't breathe." Frank's words came in sharp, wheezing gasps. "The powder . . . the powder . . ." He doubled over, his body racked by quaking spasms that drove him to his knees.

"Frank!" Gerald stepped forward to aid his former captain.

Frank's right arm raked at the air, warning his companion away. "The powder. Po–poison. Get—get away."

Poison? Gerald's brain raced. *Poison—toxin—antitoxin* . . . His eyes rolled down to the two bags in his hand— two bags of white pills marked antitoxin—while he backed away from the pile of red dust beside the now writhing captain.

In an instant his mind made the logical leap. Even though every man and woman in the fleet of Mother Ships had been immunized against all terrestrial diseases, that did not preclude the human development of a new strain of virus or bacteria deadly only to those who had come to subjugate a water-rich planet light-years from their own home world. The red dust so boldly labeled with the V of the resistance movement *was* the rumored secret weapon!

And in his hand was the antitoxin used to protect the fifth columnists who aided the rebelling humans here onplanet. Gerald's heart pounded, pumping green blood through his system until it reverberated in his temples. He saw it now! He was as certain of his deductions as he had been of anything in his life!

"Get away from him!" Gerald ordered while his fingers clawed at the plastic, ripping open one of the bags. "Stay away. They've developed a poison to use against us. Burn the house! Burn the boxes! And burn him!''

As Gerald yanked his gas mask from his nose and mouth, the Blue leader and his men opened a spray of energy bolts on the toxin-packed cottage. The blasts soon consumed the white house in flames. While Gerald gulped a single antitoxin tablet down his dry throat, the blasts swept over the now dead Frank and the boxes of toxin beside him.

"Sergeant," Gerald called to the Blue unit leader. "Take these and distribute them to as many of the men as possible. Then get the men back into the shuttles."

With one last glance at the burning cottage, Gerald turned and ran toward his own vehicle. It still wasn't too late to salvage the day. The over two hundred remaining shock troopers under his command—all immune to the resistance's V-Dust—could be the factor needed to turn away the mob now storming Visitor Security in Chicago's Loop. His promotion as well as Alicia's bed were still within his grasp—if he worked quickly.

"Get the men into the shuttles," Gerald called out before he stepped into his own craft, hastened through the interior, and settled into the pilot's couch. His fingers jabbed at a series of buttons before him on the console. Direct communications to Alicia's Mother Ship opened. "High Captain Gerald here. I have just discovered and destroyed a cache of highly toxic material the resistance intends to—"

"Too late, Gerald!" Alicia's own voice blared over the craft's intercom. "Chicago Security has fallen to the toxin."

Gerald listened in horror to his commander's thumbnail sketch of all that had occurred while he had led an attack on the abandoned resistance headquarters.

"All able fighting units are immediately ordered back to the Mother Ship," Alicia concluded. "The Supreme Commander John has ordered a withdrawal from Earth's atmosphere."

"But—but my men and I are immune," Gerald stammered while his vision of glory and power crumbled. "I can strike the Loop within minutes. I can—"

"Immediate withdrawal from all action and return to the Mother Ship," Alicia shouted. "Immediate withdrawal!"

An echoing snap, like the breaking of a limb, reverberated through the squad vessel as communication was cut from the other end. Gerald slammed a fist against the side of the couch. A string of curses in his native tongue spewed from makeup-disguised lips. He had been so close to success, to assuring his steady climb to power, *real power*, within Alicia's forces. So close!

"Troops are within the shuttles," a voice said over his earphone.

Gerald sat straight. His hands reached out and took the craft's controls. Immediate withdrawal and return to the Mother Ship were his orders, and he intended to obey them. He had made enough mistakes this morning.

"Secure for liftoff," he ordered over intership communications, waited thirty seconds for the troops to prepare themselves, then he eased his shuttle craft back into the air, heading for the silver-blue saucer that still hung above the heart of Chicago.

An hour later, a fleet of fifty Visitor Mother Ships shot from Earth's atmosphere into the darkness of space. Below, cheering crowds watched and celebrated. Earth had met, faced, and defeated the first alien threat to come from the stars—all because of a simple child's toy and some red dust it carried inside.

Chapter Two

Samuel Walker strapped a razor-honed, sheathed stiletto above his right ankle. Dropping the cuff of his black pants leg to conceal the weapon, he stood and slipped a .32-caliber snub-nosed revolver into a clip holster. This he hid at the small of his back inside the waist of his trousers.

Grabbing a black turtleneck sweater tossed across a lumpy, springless cot, Walker poked his arms through the sleeves, pulled it over his head, and gave the collar a half roll downward. Carefully he arranged the loose fold of fabric at the bottom of the sweater to hide the revolver's bulge. Satisfied with the position of cloth and weapon, he lifted a black belt from the cot and tightened it around his waist.

From the belt dangled the first line of defense in the small arsenal of weapons he carried—a holstered .45-caliber automatic and a sheathed hunting knife that had a seven-inch blade with an inch of sharpened false edge running along its top. The revolver and stiletto were snugly hidden, just in case.

Walker caught a glimpse of himself in a jagged mirror

fragment hanging on a scarred, bare wooden wall. Pursing his lips, he gave a dubious shake of his head. He looked as if he had just escaped from Alfred Hitchcock's—

His mind went blank; he couldn't recall the name of the movie he had seen so many times on late-night television. It starred Cary Grant as a former cat burglar. Grace Kelly was Grant's romantic interest, he remembered as the plot of the movie rolled through his mind. But he couldn't drag up the movie's title.

Comes from being locked away in this damned stall for too long, Sam Walker, he told himself. *You're beginning to forget what the* real *world was like.*

With a so-what-does-it-matter shrug to the mirror's reflection, Walker turned to glimpse the alluring dance of two very bare and very swollen-looking breasts as Kathleen Wagner pulled a black turtleneck over her head. The bottom of the sweater hung on the budlike thickness of her coral-hued nipples for an instant before the fabric dropped to veil the sleekness of her body.

"Quit your grinning, Mister. And close your mouth. You're starting to drool." Kathleen's hazel eyes rolled to him with mock exasperation as she patted stray strands of her dark walnut hair into place. "After six months together, I'd think you'd be bored with cheap thrills!"

"Still making up for those first seven weeks when you were playing hard to get? Give me another sixty or seventy years to get bored."

Walker leaned toward the tall, statuesque woman. The kiss he intended for her cheek slid an inch downward and planted itself firmly on her lips. Her arms encircled him. Her mouth opened, and her tongue rushed to greet his. The enthusiasm took him by surprise. After all, they had just spent two hours making love while they waited for the summer sun to drop beneath the horizon.

"Mmm," Kathleen purred when she slowly eased from

him. "Enough of that or we'll never get our shopping done tonight."

A wry smile lifted the corners of Walker's mouth. He reached down, grabbed a second belt with a .45 and hunting blade strung on its length, and handed it to the black-clad beauty. Kathleen had a way with euphemisms. Here they were, living in a horse stall in the middle of the stable area of the abandoned Arlington Park Race Track, they carried more heavy artillery than he ever had during his years in Vietnam, they were about to slink into the night to scrounge what they needed to stay alive from deserted supermarkets, and Kathleen described their venture as *shopping*.

"You get the door and I'll get the lights." Buckling the belt about her slim waist, Kathleen crossed the stall to three unscented candles burning atop a footlocker.

Shopping! Walker's smile widened while he moved to the door created when he had nailed the two-part stall door together during his first week of hiding, and unlatched it. That Kathleen could find levity in their day-to-day survival rituals was nothing short of a miracle. At times she and her undaunted sense of humor were all that kept him from climbing the walls.

Waiting until he nodded, Kathleen bent and blew out the candles. If she ever thought he was overcautious in his rule that the door should never be opened with a light burning inside, she never mentioned it. Nor had she objected when he had lined the interior of the stall with black construction plastic to eliminate the possibility of light radiating out through cracks in the walls and drawing the unwanted attention of reptilian eyes.

Besides, the plastic helped cut the smell, Walker thought, remembering how ineffectual the disinfectant and lime he had spread over the stall's floor had been. The ancient odor of horse manure and urine, permanently implanted in soil and wood over years of racing seasons, constantly hung in the air. The unsavory nature of the abandoned thoroughbred racecourse was one of the main reasons he had chosen it as a hiding place.

"What's our choice tonight? Rolling Meadows, Palatine, or Arlington Heights?" Kathleen whispered as she moved through the door Walker opened. "I understand there's a new Hunan restaurant in Palantine. Want to give it a try?"

"We slip across Northwest Highway, hit the supermarket, and get back here as soon as possible." Walker lifted two burlap bags from the wall when he walked from the stall and handed her one.

"I was hoping we could make it to a bookstore. I've gotten hooked on MacDonald's Travis McGee stories."

"We'll have to make do with the book spinners at the supermarket tonight," Walker insisted as they stepped from beneath the shedrow and into the light of a full moon. "Can't shake that nagging feeling at the back of my mind."

Walker's gaze rose to the sky. For the fifth night in a row an unobscured panorama of stars burned in the heavens. The Visitors' Mother Ship no longer floated over Chicago, its oblate spheroid form no longer blotting out half the sky.

Only twice in the months Walker had been trapped in the Chicago area had the gargantuan spacecraft left its position above the city. On both occasions it had been gone for a single night. As restless as it had made him to have the city-sized ship constantly hovering over him, it only tripled his disquiet having it gone and not knowing why it had left or where it was.

"Think we should pick up some batteries for the radio?" Kathleen turned from the empty sky to face him.

"It wouldn't hurt." Walker started down the row of long, deserted barns whose vacant stalls had once held some of the finest racing stock in the country. "But I doubt if we'll learn anything."

The only news that made it on the air was carefully screened by the aliens, then parroted by their official human spokesperson Kristine Walsh. Kathleen and he had tossed their portable radio into a corner after several weeks of unsuccessfully trying to glean any real information about the Visitors' activities from the Chicago broadcasts. Sony Walkmans scrounged from abandoned electronics stores and a wealth of tapes from deserted shops provided far more stimulating listening.

"Could they have emptied Chicago and moved on to another city, Sam?" Kathleen reached out and took his hand, her fingers trembling.

"They're fast, but not that fast." Walker tried to inject confidence into his words, but the flatness of his tone fell far short of reassuring.

Both Kathleen and he knew how fast the Visitors eliminated the populations of towns when they decided to move. Kathleen knew better than he, as she had escaped the Visitors by hiding in a trunk in her cellar the night the shock troopers raided Arlington Heights. She had believed that she was the only one left in the Chicago suburb until Walker discovered her cowering in an aisle of a deserted grocery two weeks later.

That day they had joined together for mutual survival. Seven weeks later they became lovers. Six months had passed since that accidental meeting. Walker considered them husband and wife, although no official marriage vows had ever been spoken nor even mentioned. Certain things between a woman and man never need words, he realized. Other bonds existed than those on paper, stronger, more permanent ones that stemmed from the heart and soul.

"I wish we'd hear from Janus." Kathleen ducked beneath the inside railing of a small training track and headed across the field at its center. "Do you think something's happened to him?"

"The old codger can take care of himself. No need to worry about him," Walker answered, trying to edge aside his own doubts.

Janus Brodaski was a sixty-year-old observer for the Chicago resistance movement who kept surveillance of Visitor activity in the abandoned northwest suburbs. A crusty veteran of the Polish freedom fighters during World War II, Janus had hidden Walker after an unsuccessful attempt to penetrate the Visitor security net west of Palatine. Walker wouldn't be alive tonight if it weren't for Janus.

"It's been nine days since he last made contact." The concern furrowing Kathleen's brow was evident even in the dim moonlight. "He usually checks on us every three days. He's like clockwork."

"Maybe the resistance gave him a new assignment." Walker reached out and gave her shoulder a reassuring squeeze. "The old man knows his way around. Surely they have more important things for him to do than keeping tabs on people like us."

Kathleen offered no reply, ducked under the railing on the opposite side of the training track to move west along a high chain-link fence that enclosed the racetrack. Two hundred yards along the barrier of webbed steel, she paused beside an eroded drainage ditch. Without a word, her head turned to each side, then she scanned the sky above. Certain their movements went unobserved, she dropped into the ditch and crawled beneath the fence.

How much she's changed in a few short months, Walker thought as he watched her stand and cautiously survey their surroundings again. He could discern no trace of the frightened legal secretary he had found six months ago.

Their life together, the existence of night scavengers struggling to survive from one day to the next, constantly prepared to face death at alien hands, had given her a confidence, a strength that had been lacking in Kathleen

Wagner, legal secretary. He smiled while he followed her under the fence. *The lady's a street-wise survivor, able to take care of herself even if I weren't here. Changed, definitely changed.*

The thought Walker had repressed since the morning wriggled from the back of his mind when he stood and picked his way across a railroad track on the other side of the fence. Kathleen's latest change left his gut twisted and knotted. She was pregnant. A month, maybe two, she had recently announced, supporting her statement with the fact that she had missed two periods.

Walker's joy, his hugs and kisses of delight, had only been a half lie. A child, their child, was something he dreamed of—a son or daughter, it didn't matter. But . . .

But not now. Not now! Walker tried to shove his doubts away, but they refused to be moved. A world overrun with reptilian invaders from another star system was no place for a child. What kind of life could he give it? A child needed the warm sunlight to grow, not an existence of creeping among the shadows, stealing food from abandoned stores.

A more immediate problem, he realized, was that there was no way they could keep an infant concealed in their stable hideaway. Babies, no matter how angelic to their parents, cried. Those cries would eventually draw unwanted attention.

"Certain I can't convince you to go into town?" Kathleen turned to him when they reached a wide ribbon of concrete bearing the name Northwest Highway.

"The supermarket and the supermarket only." Walker's answer held a sharp edge Kathleen did not deserve. His frustration stemmed from the circumstances which robbed him of being a normal husband and father.

Two black-clad shadows within the shadows of the night, they scurried across the highway and crouched beside the overgrown scrubbery of a deserted fast-food restaurant.

After a quick check to once again assure themselves they weren't being watched, they started west, darting from service station to auto shop to insurance agency.

Changes—nothing but damned changes! Nothing's permanent. Nothing! Walker could not contain the bitterness that churned within him. His life had been one drastic change after another—changes over which he had no control.

Uncle Sam had thrown him the first curve ball when he was eighteen. His lottery number had come up. A college freshman one moment, he was snatched up by the back of his shaggy-haired neck and tossed down in the middle of Vietnam to pilot a Huey Cobra. Like it or not, he learned to survive in that rotor-bladed deathship of the air, and survived while others went home in plastic bags or vanished forever in the jungles of Southeast Asia.

In 1975 Uncle Sam jerked him up again, flung him across the Pacific, and challenged him to survive once again, this time in a place he had once called home, a land as hostile and deadly as Vietnam's rice paddies. Only now he was robbed of uniform, weapons, and chopper.

Didn't do too good a job of that. He grimaced, remembering the years he spent drifting from one city to another, unable to bring his life into focus. Even now those countless days remained a blur in his mind.

In Los Angeles he hadn't been sure why he had come to the West Coast, but he found a job as a commercial pilot of a helicopter taxi service. This was another major change— from bum to gainfully employed member of society. He also rediscovered college. Night courses at UCLA sharpened his focus. In five years he garnered a degree in electrical engineering.

A week after he received his diploma, the Visitors and their gigantic ships arrived. He had been as excited about the alien friends from distant Sirius as the next man. The

knowledge they promised could bring the changes humankind had needed for centuries.

A job interview had brought him to Chicago. While
employing a six-pack of beer to drown the disappointment
over not getting that job, he watched the first television
broadcasts of the "scientists' conspiracy" against the
Visitors. The rumors of an underground attack by scientists
closed down local airports to all but "official" travel before
he could return to Los Angeles. The same security reasons
locked in rail and bus transportation.

Only when Walker had rented a car and attempted to
drive from Chicago did he fully recognize the extent of the
Visitors' control. Every artery to and from the city was
roadblocked. The Visitors had turned Chicago into an
isolated island in a matter of a few weeks—and he was
trapped on that island.

Five times he had tried to walk from the city, to wriggle
through the ring of Visitor security. It was easy enough to
make it from the heart of Chicago and slip through the
barren suburbs, whose missing populations were ignored by
Chicagoans. Yet each time he encountered an impenetrable
barrier—a tight-knit line of red-uniformed shock troopers
cordoning off the city from the rest of the world.

On his last attempt to break through the barrier, he had
been discovered. The Visitors had given chase, but Janus
Brodaski had stepped from the shadows and provided an
escape via an old warehouse and a maintenance tunnel that
ran beneath it.

Janus had attempted to recruit him into the resistance, but
Walker had taken refuge in the stable area of deserted
Arlington Park instead. He was a survivor who had fought
one thankless war for his country; he had no intention of
repeating that mistake. Better to just hole up until everything blew over.

Blew over. Walker shook his head. Kathleen's pregnancy

threw him back into the thick of things. If they were to continue to be survivors, if they were to raise the child now growing in her belly, they had to find a way through the Visitor sentries and seek refuge in the relative security of the country.

To do that, Walker needed Janus. Somehow the resistance was able to move through the sentries. Janus could show them the way. *If only Janus were here.*

"It looks clear to me." Kathleen's voice intruded into his thoughts.

Walker's head jerked around. Silently he thanked the darkness for hiding the chagrin on his face. He had been so lost in thought he had forgotten where they were, the danger they faced.

Poking his head around the corner of an empty car wash, he peered at the wide parking lot that stretched before them. Nothing. Nor did he see the familiar silhouette of a Visitor squad vehicle hovering above the supermarket at the end of the open field of concrete.

Once, for an entire week a Visitor squad had been posted around the supermarket to trap stragglers like themselves. On numerous occasions a shuttle, flying lights out, simply hung in the night sky over the store for the same purpose.

Walker had no doubt the lizards knew they were hiding near, but he had no intention of being found. This was only one of the supermarkets they regularly raided. If guards were posted in one place, he and Kathleen would sink back and move on to another store.

"All clear," Walker said as he pulled back into the shadows. "Ready?"

Kathleen nodded, and the two sprinted across the parking lot. They stopped only when the shadows of the building cloaked them. Another check of the area and they edged around the building, opened a window at the rear of the store, and crawled inside. With burlap sacks in hand, they hastened through a storage area into the supermarket.

"I'll hit the fruit and vegetables. You get the meats. Meet you at the hardware section to pick up batteries in five minutes," Kathleen whispered. She took a step, then looked back at Walker. "And, Sam, get more than just beef stew. Even cold corned-beef hash would be a nice change."

Before he could protest, she darted down an aisle to the right. Walker shrugged and moved to the left.

The store was one of those discount groceries that had grown up during the recession of the late '70s. It was nothing but row upon row of canned goods, many still packed in cardboard boxes. The lack of fresh produce and meat had once made such stores distasteful to him. Now the deserted supermarket was a treasure trove of tidily canned, unspoiled food.

Reaching the meat section, he selected cans of tuna, salmon, boneless chicken, corned-beef hash, and, of course, his favorite, beef stew. He slung the half-full bag over his shoulder and hurried on to the hardware aisle where Kathleen stood examining a display of dry-cell batteries.

"Does the radio use D or C batteries?" she asked when he stopped at her side.

"Can't remember," Walker replied. "Take a couple packages of—"

His whispered words were drowned by a booming voice that echoed through the abandoned store.

"I can hear you shaking, rabbits! I know you're in there! There's no need to hide! Come out, my rabbits! Come out!"

Thoughts of batteries were forgotten as Walker and Kathleen tugged automatics free from the holsters on their hips and pivoted. The front entrance of the store gaped wide. From it a single beam of light sliced through the darkness, seeking them.

Chapter Three

To be alone with Commander Alicia in her private
quarters had been one of Gerald's fondest fantasies since the
fleet first left its home world. But not this way!

His carefully nurtured dream included visions of Alicia
and him exploring the erotic avenues of their bodies
between the clinging sheets of her bed. Instead, he stood at
rigid attention before the Mother Ship commander's desk
while Alicia scanned a computer display that scrolled a
summary of the reports from the ship's biological research
team. From the way she busied a human-disguised hand
through a shoulder-length cascade of blonde hair, he was
certain the reports were stacked against him.

A blip of light from a viewscreen on the wall behind
Alicia's desk drew his attention. Gerald risked shifting his
eyes from his commander to the screen. There the vessel's
optical sensors provided a wide-angle view of the Visitor
fleet—fifty gargantuan Mother Ships grouped like cowering
rodents behind Earth's single moon. Only the Los Angeles
Mother Ship had not escaped Earth's atmosphere. That
damnable television newsman Michael Donovan and the

fifth column traitor Martin had captured the vessel. As to the fate of Diana, who had commanded the ship, no one was certain.

Hiding, Gerald thought with bitterness. The fleet was doing nothing more than hiding. The great ships were unable to return to Earth because of the bacteria the resistance fighters had released into the atmosphere. Nor could they return to Sirius. The Great Leader waited there; none of the fleet's officers desired to face his wrath for their failure.

Gerald watched the blip of light, a shuttle crossing from one Mother Ship to another. At the moment, he would have traded his high captain's stripes for those of a private if he could be on board that shuttle. If he could be anywhere other than in Alicia's private quarters.

"High Captain Gerald," Alicia began as her cold blue eyes rolled up to look at him, "everything here indicates I have but one choice in dealing with your stupidity. You should be jettisoned into space with the rest of the garbage aboard—without the benefit of a space suit."

In spite of his attempt to remain calm and collected, Gerald swallowed. The worst he had expected was to have his rank stripped and a lifetime assignment in the ship's septic tanks. Alicia had just pronounced a death sentence!

"Fear, Gerald! I can smell it on you now. The same fear that ruled you during the attack on the resistance's headquarters!" Alicia made no attempt at the awkward syllables of English now, but spat out her words in their native tongue. "You held the key to defeating the rebels in your hands. But your own worthless life was more important to you than our task—more important than Our Great Leader, than saving our people and our world!"

"I distributed the antitoxin to my men." Gerald's mind raced desperately, scrambling for an argument to sway Alicia's death sentence. "With two hundred immune shock troopers, I could have defeated the humans who attacked our Chicago Security headquar—"

"You sought to save your own life, fool!" Alicia hammered a fist atop her desk. "With those two sacks of antitoxin, my scientists could have reproduced it! With just *one* of those tablets everyone in the fleet would carry the immunity now held in your body. But your fear of death, your cowardly fear, destroyed that!"

Gerald tried to speak. The dryness of his throat and mouth left his forked tongue immobile.

Alicia jabbed a finger at the computer display screen. "For five days my top biologists have tried to isolate the antitoxin within the systems of your men. Each attempt has ended in total failure—as well as in the death of seven ablebodied soldiers. Once in our bloodstreams, the effects of the antitoxin are observable, but our scientists can't isolate the agent itself!"

She glared at Gerald, her eyes narrow and her mouth a thin, tight line. "Many of my advisers have suggested that it would be suitable if you volunteered as test case for the antitoxin research."

"If that is what is required of me." Gerald forced himself to speak, unable to conceal a quaver in his voice. "I have only sought to serve Our Great Leader."

Alicia ignored him. "In spite of your craven actions, all may not be lost. If Earth's scientists created an antitoxin, our scientists will eventually be able to duplicate their efforts. One day we will return to Earth and make it ours."

She paused. Her head turned to the viewscreen. For heavy minutes she stared at the clustered Mother Ships poised motionless behind the dark side of the moon.

"I refuse to just sit here and wait for that day to come," she said when she looked back at Gerald. "I have a plan to pave a way for our return, one that will bring Our Great

Leader's smile. A plan that will provide a method for you to redeem yourself, Gerald.''

"I stand ready to serve in whatever capacity required." Gerald's pulse doubled its pace. Alicia offered him an alternative to death. Whatever she wanted, he would be only too willing to perform.

"There are those still on Earth who will aid us." A pleased smile uplifted the corners of her mouth. "There are even members of the Chicago resistance who will serve us—those we have converted. It will be your task to rally our allies on Earth, Gerald. You and your immune shock troopers will be the key I need to once more unlock Earth to us."

Alicia motioned Gerald closer to her desk. Her fingers tapped over the computer's keyboard, then she swiveled the screen around for his eyes.

"I have already made radio contact with one of our Chicago converts. Your first task will be to meet with him. A squad vehicle awaits you in bay one. You'll leave as soon as I've completed your briefing."

Gerald watched and listened, carefully concealing the self-satisfaction that gradually replaced the fear that dominated him but a few minutes ago. Not only did Alicia offer him a reprise to his death sentence, she gave him the route to continue his rise within her ranks!

Chapter Four

Walker crouched in the center of the aisle to avoid the single beam of light that swept back and forth through the darkness of the deserted supermarket. Leveling his .45 automatic at the end of the aisle, he waited. Beside him, Kathleen imitated his action, her position reversed to cover a rear attack.

"My little rabbits, you can come out now," the booming voice reverberated through the abandoned grocery. "There is no need to hide. I saw you sneak in here."

Edging back a step, Walker leaned to Kathleen's ear. "Damned lizards are probably all over the place. If we're going to make a break for it, the back door will give us a better shot at reaching cover. We'd never make it across the parking lot out front."

The deep voice boomed out once more. "Come, come, my little rabbits. There is no need to be frightened. This is no time to play hide and seek."

When Walker turned to lead the retreat to the supermarket's storeroom, Kathleen's hand reached out to halt him. She whispered, "Sam, that's no Visitor. Listen. The words don't hiss or echo." She cocked her head to the side. The taunting voice rang out once more. "Dammit, Sam, I think it's Janus."

"Janus?" Walker listened, realizing that in the months they had known the old Polish freedom fighter they had never heard the man call out—or even heard him speak in normal conversational tones. Whenever they had spoken, it had always been in hushed, guarded whispers.

"You rabbits can come out now!" The man's voice rent the store's silence again. "There is no need for hiding. The snakes are gone! We drove the slimy bastards away!"

Kathleen was right; Walker was certain of it. He discerned just a trace of an accent in the man's words. Cautiously he stood, prepared to duck at the first sign of trouble. "Janus? Is that you?"

"Who the hell do you think it is?" The beam shifted, spotlighting Walker's face. "Think one of those scaly lizards would come in here shouting like this?"

There was a metallic click and the harsh light died. Footsteps echoed on the store's dusty floor, moving toward Walker's position. Janus Brodaski's familiar form appeared at the end of the aisle. The light flashed on again, this time to illuminate Janus's face for a moment.

"You're lucky Kathleen or I didn't put a couple of holes in that beer belly of yours, Janus," Walker reprimanded the resistance observer as he approached. "You should know better than to break in on us like that. And that damned flashlight! Are you crazy? You'll have the Visitors down on us in—"

"*Visitors?*" Janus edged back a sweat-stained navy blue baseball cap adorned with the familiar white outlined red C of the Chicago Cubs. Wavy strands of snow-white hair slipped out from beneath the cap. "Didn't you hear me? I say the damned snakes are gone! Got them with the V-Dust, we did! Should have been with us, Sam. Thousands of balloons filled with lizard-killing germs flying up to the sky just as pretty as you please. It was a sight a man could tell his grandchil—"

"Gone?" This from Kathleen who stared at the older man in disbelief. "The Visitors are gone?"

"Five days now." Janus's grin spread from ear to ear. "Didn't you two notice the Mother Ship was gone? It will not be back either. We put enough poison in the air to keep them away from our world forever!"

"Gone!" Kathleen's arms went around Walker's neck. She hugged him close while tears streamed down her face. "Did you hear that, Sam? They're gone. God, they're gone. Gone!"

Walker saw the strength of long, hard months disappear from her slender body. Gently he sank to the floor with her, holding her tightly as she allowed herself the luxury of shedding the tears that had been locked within for far too long.

"You should have been there, Sam." Janus lowered himself to the floor and sat cross-legged in front of the couple. He arranged the flashlight beam so that it bounced off the display of batteries to bathe them in soft light. "It was magnificent! They never knew what hit them until it was too late."

Walker cuddled Kathleen close, ignoring Janus's second reference to his absence during the fighting. The old man constantly tried to sink barbs into him because of his refusal to join Chicago's resistance movement. Even now, Janus couldn't see that Walker had made the right choice. The Visitors and their reign of terror had blown over. Kathleen and he had survived!

"Poison—red, snake-killing poison—is what did it," Janus went on, and Walker listened, piecing together the story of the toxin's development, distribution, and final use.

"A V-Day like no other. It's a shame you missed it because you were hidden away like rabbits in a smelly hole."

"What about the rest of the world?" Kathleen asked, wiping at her eyes. "The Visitors, have they abandoned the whole planet?"

"Gone. Everywhere, they are gone. Sent them running back to their own world with their scaly tails between their legs." Janus's grin faded. "The world they left is not pretty. Chicago bears the scars of war. And there is looting. Probably the same everywhere else."

"Probably?" Walker arched an eyebrow.

"We are not certain." Janus wearily shook his head. "The Visitors disrupted everything, including communications. Most of our satellites are gone. Destroyed them while they were here or as they left. No one is sure."

Walker sucked at his teeth. With communications satellites blasted from space, all electronic means of communications would be minimal and restricted to governmental use. Walker frowned. If, that is, government still existed.

"Paul Nordine has us—those who served under him on V-Day—working with what remains of Chicago's city officials," Janus continued. "We have kept the power and water plants running, but there is a problem in getting enough food into the city. The Visitors controlled the transportation lines. Neither the turcks nor trains are running."

Walker drew a deep breath, trying to place himself in Nordine's shoes. The resistance leader had taken on a task equal to his fight against the Visitors. Putting a city the size of Chicago back together would be a full-time job—especially for a man who had been a plumber before the Visitor fleet encircled the world.

"And there are problems getting medical supplies," Janus said. "Most of the hospitals are overflowing."

"What about all those aboard the Mother Ships? The men

and women the Visitors processed for food?'' Walker interrupted his friend.

"Still on the snakes' ships,'' Janus's eyes rolled to the floor and his shoulders slumped forward. "There was no way we could get—''

"No!'' Kathleen's head moved from side to side with determination. "I don't want to hear it. Not tonight. Please. Tonight is a time to celebrate. The Visitors are gone. That's enough for now.''

Janus's smile returned, and he nodded with understanding. "Yes, of course. I must be going.''

"Going?'' Kathleen stared at him. "Aren't you going to celebrate with us?''

"I cannot spend my night here.'' Janus's smile widened, and he shook his head. "There are pockets of rabbits like you two here and there who must be told the good news. It is time everybody came back out into the sunlight! Even all the little rabbits.''

"And what about little Cubbies.'' Walker tilted his head to Janus's cap when they stood. "Will the Cubs come out of their cellar too?''

"Cellar?'' Janus's blue eyes sparked with the defensive fire of a diehard Cubs fan. "If lizards have a hell, then that is but one more sin the Visitors will burn for!''

"There's always next year.'' Walker gave Janus's shoulder a sympathetic pat while they walked to the store's front door. The Cubs were a game behind the division-leading Mets, and serious National League pennant contenders for the second year in a row since 1945—the year they lost the World Series to the Detroit Tigers—when the Visitors had halted all human sporting events. Walker repeated the familiar refrain of Cubs fans: "There's always next year.''

Janus grunted as he opened the door to a battered lime-green Ford Pinto and slipped behind the wheel. He glanced up at Walker and Kathleen. "Celebrate tonight. Tomorrow I will be back to talk with you. We need help in the city."

Arms around each other's waists, they stood and watched the old man wheel from the empty parking lot and trundle westward toward Palatine on Northwest Highway. When the lightless car disappeared in the darkness, Walker pulled Kathleen close, his mouth covering hers.

"The man said celebrate," Walker whispered when their lips parted. "Have you any suggestions?"

"I'll come up with something by the time we get back." Kathleen coyly kissed his cheek and traced circles on his chest with a finger. "If I can't, I'm sure you'll think of something."

He grinned, leaned forward for another kiss, then abruptly stood straight. "Wait right here. I'll be back." He darted into the dark supermarket.

"Sam?" Kathleen called after him.

"Wait there. I just thought of something for our celebration!"

Two minutes later he trotted from the abandoned building. The two sacks they had forgotten were tossed over his shoulder. Handing Kathleen one, he wrapped an arm about her waist and started back toward Arlington Park with the woman he loved hugging his side.

His gaze rose to the unobscured sky as though to reassure himself the Visitors' great Mother Ship was truly gone. *Gone! Gone forever!* Janus's words rolled over in his mind. Kathleen and he could have a life together—a real life.

So will our child. He grinned and gave Kathleen a long, tight squeeze before letting her crawl back under the fence. *No life of nights and shadows for Samuel Walker's kid!* He watched Kathleen stand, suddenly realizing there wouldn't be a kid unless he asked a question that had been unnecessary when the night began.

"You know what I think we should do tomorrow when

Janus comes back?" he asked while he ducked under the fence. "We should see if the old man can find us a preacher or a priest or somebody to make an honest woman out of you."

Kathleen turned and gazed up at him. "Sam Walker, was that a proposal?"

"I'll do it on my knees if that's what it takes to get a yes from you." Walker hugged her close again. "Think you could stand growing old with someone like me?"

"Yes. And yes," she answered both his questions, then stretched upward on tiptoes to cut off further comments with a loud, sloppy kiss mixed with fresh tears of happiness.

Clinging to one another, they walked between the long rows of barns, this time caring little whether the shadows cloaked their movements. When they reached the first of two asphalt roads that divided the track's stable area, Kathleen halted and glanced toward the grandstand and the main track. She shoved her burlap bag into Walker's arms and turned to him.

"Sam, this might sound silly, but I want some flowers for our celebration tonight."

"Tell me where and I'll get them," he answered. "But there aren't many florists open in this part of the city."

"There are flowers blooming in the center field of the track." She smiled. "You take the groceries back to the stall. I'm going to pick the finest bouquet you've ever seen!"

"Want some company?" he asked.

"I don't want to hurt your feelings, not tonight," she answered cautiously, "but I'd like to be alone with someone else for a while. I have a lot of things to thank him for tonight."

Walker gently kissed her cheek and nodded. "Mention me in your prayers while you're having that talk. And remember, I like tulips."

Returning his kiss, she trotted toward the main race-course with a wide grin on her face. The grin was catching, Walker realized as he showed his own toothy smile. But then it was a night for grinning and laughing. They deserved to be happy and more.

Walker hastened back to the stall that had sheltered them for months. Now they had a chance at getting that *more*. Changes atop of changes, he thought, but this time life had dealt a winning hand to Samuel Walker.

Inside he set the two sacks aside, then dragged a card table to the center of the room and covered it with a piece of linen Kathleen had taken from a fabric store. His grin grew as he placed two folding chairs on opposite ends of the table. It wasn't an elegant setting, but then he wasn't through.

His rush back into the supermarket had secured more than their forgotten bags. Reaching into his sack, he withdrew two long, white, tapered candles and two glass candle holders. Carefully wedging the candles into the holders, he set them atop the table and lit them with a match.

Next he extracted a bottle of domestic champagne from the bag and placed it at the center of the table. Neither Kathleen nor he had allowed themselves the luxury of alcohol since taking refuge in the stable. The single bottle would probably leave them both reeling.

Stepping back to eye the setting, he smiled. For an instant he toyed with the idea of placing a can of beef stew before each chair, then let the idea pass. Tonight was too special to mar with even a small bad joke. After all, he had asked a woman to marry him. Better, she had accepted.

With a final admiring gaze at his handiwork, Walker walked to the door. He paused at the threshold, hands going to the heavily laden belt about his waist. He shrugged, unbuckled the belt, and tossed the holstered .45 and hunting knife atop the cot. He then tugged the revolver from the small of his back and threw it to the bed. Last, he unstrapped the stiletto below his calf and dropped it atop the small arsenal.

The hint of an ironic smile moved on his lips when he turned to the door once again. The same naked sensation he had experienced for weeks after his return from Vietnam suffused him now. During the months of hiding, the knives and pistols had become as much a part of his attire as his pants—maybe more so. A pair of breeches wouldn't stop a two-legged lizard from Sirius.

If all that Janus had said about Chicago was true, Kathleen and he might be carrying added protection for months before they permanently packed the pistols away. Walker edged the thought aside. He'd worry about the rest of the world tomorrow. Tonight was special, and .45-caliber automatics had no place in it.

Outside he carefully closed the stall door, partially from habit, mostly to conceal from Kathleen the surprise waiting inside. He turned and started toward the grandstand and the sandy, oval racetrack stretched before it. While he had no intention of disturbing Kathleen's private moment, he could meet her by the track's outside rail and walk her back to the stall.

Kathleen with flowers in her arm . . . Kathleen in evening gown and a suggestive trace of perfume about her . . . Kathleen with their child in her arms . . . He shook his head while he passed through one barn and headed toward another. The images he called up were so distant from the black-clad Kathleen he had lived with for half a year.

There's so much we still have to learn about one another. He rubbed at his right jaw, trying to massage a dull ache that settled around his molars. *But, then, there's no rush. We have a lifetime together.*

Increasing the pressure of the heel of his palm against his

jaw, he winced. The ache vibrated through his lower teeth, then tingled upward, moving from the back of his mouth to his front teeth.

"Damn!" He paused between barns and worked both hands at the back of his jaw.

A year had passed since he last visited a dentist, but a cavity, even a big one, couldn't cause an ache that set every tooth in his head to throbbing. Several times in Vietnam when a chopper's rotor pitch was just right, his whole mouth would throb. He hadn't felt this sensation in years. The closest thing to it was—

Walker froze. Ice formed about his heart.

—the day the Visitors' Mother Ship had first appeared over Los Angeles!

His head jerked up, remembering the week it had taken to accustom himself to the vibrations produced by the alien craft's gravity drive. The ice floe within his chest closed.

There above the tops of the barns skimmed a Visitor squad vehicle. Like a giant wingless insect it silently shot overhead, moonlight agleam along its segmented white body.

How? Walker's mind railed. The toxin, V-Dust—Janus said the Visitors had been driven away, had returned to their own world! How could a shuttle be here? *How?*

His aching teeth forgotten, he ran. From one barn to the next he sprinted, following the course the ship had taken. As he darted from the final stable bordering a wide parking lot that separated the barn area from the track itself, he skidded to a halt. In the next instant he leaped back into the concealing shadows.

Breath short, heart pounding, and eyes wide, he stared as the Visitor shuttle silently drifted down to land at the center of the barren concrete. Its door opened, top swinging up, while the lowered portion formed a ramp to the ground.

Walker's right hand crept to his waist and closed around empty air. He had left his weapons on top of the cot!

Lights, the beams of two headlights, flared alive to the left. The rumble of a starting motor followed an instant later. He leaned forward to watch a dark car ease from between two barns to the north and pull beside the shuttle. As the driver stepped from the car, eleven red-uniformed shock troopers, each holding an angular rifle, walked from the vessel. Ten of the Visitors encircled the car and shuttle while the eleventh approached the car's driver.

Walker's eyes darted from side to side. There was no way he could get closer. The only thing between him and the open parking lot was a low, white-washed wooden fence. Even if he could make it to the fence without being seen, he still wouldn't be close enough to hear the words passing between human and alien.

His gaze returned to the center of the lot. The glow of a parking light reflected off a license plate proudly proclaiming Illinois "The Land of Lincoln" beneath the numbers 049-ESB. He was unable to tell the car's make or its color in the dimness of the moonlight.

While he watched, the Visitor beside the car reached out and squeezed the driver's shoulder. Together they walked around the vehicle toward the still open door.

How? The question repeated over and over in Walker's mind. How could the reptilian Visitors breathe an atmosphere contaminated with the red toxin? Unless Janus had lied to them about the Visitors' defeat.

He shook his head. The old Polish freedom fighter would never betray them. These eleven snakes were different, somehow immune to the toxin. But how? The nagging question remained.

As the car's driver slid behind the wheel again, one of the guards shouted. His arm shot toward the racetrack. Eleven rifles swung about.

No! Walker's mind screamed when his gaze followed those deadly muzzles eastward. *Kathleen!*

Her arms cradling a multihued bouquet, Kathleen ducked beneath the track's outside rail and started down a grassy embankment skirting the parking lot. She took two strides and froze. Her head lifted. She stared at the grounded shuttle before her. The blossoms tumbled from her arms as her right hand dropped to the .45 strapped to her hip.

"Nooooo!"

Walker's scream drowned in the sizzling hiss of eleven rifles. Bolts of intense blue sliced through the night as burning pearls of light shot out at her.

One . . . two . . . five . . . ten . . . He lost count of the flaring globes of death that struck Kathleen's vulnerable body. Like a mannequin with a madman yanking its strings, she jerked and twisted under the impacts, spinning about with arms flying wildly before she crumpled facedown in the grass.

Paralyzed with horror, brain numb yet writhing in torment, Walker stared in mute agony while flickering flames died out at the places where the bolts had struck. He heard the cough of a motor starting. His jaw felt the vibrations of the shuttle. But his eyes remained on the oh-so-still form sprawled on the embankment.

Like a man lost in a nightmare, Walker stumbled from the barn's shadows and managed to crawl over the low fence. His feet seemed to hasten forward of their own volition.

"Kathleen." His voice came as a soft whisper that rose to a howling cry of agony. "Kathleen!"

He ran now, unaware of the world around him. His whole being focused on the still form of the woman he loved. "No! Kathleen, nooooo!"

Dropping to his knees in the dew-moistened grass, he reached down. He lifted her into his arms, hugging her close, trying to infuse a portion of the life pumping through his veins into her lifeless breast.

Dead. Tears welled from his eyes and rolled down his cheeks. His body racked with uncontrollable shudders. In one instant a lifetime stretched before them; the next— nothing! *How? God, How?*

His head rose, and he stared over the now empty parking lot. The Visitor shuttle was gone. He blinked. Hadn't they seen him? Why hadn't they cut him down too? Why was he allowed to live?

His gaze shifted from the sky. In the distance, he saw the taillights of a car pulling from Arlington Park's stable area. Numbers he had only casually glanced at now burned vividly in his mind. 049-ESB—a number he would never forget!

With Kathleen's limp body in his arms, Samuel Walker stood and walked toward the shadowy rows of barns.

Chapter Five

Sam Walker knelt and meticulously replanted the flowers he had so carefully removed from a small plot at the center of Arlington Park's center field. When the last tulip bulb lay buried six inches beneath the rich soil, he stood and brushed his dirty hands on the thighs of his pants.

His gaze traced over the flower-covered mound, inspecting his work. The rains would eventually repack the earth he had disturbed. In a year the mound would be indiscernible.

"Did you make a marker?" Janus Brodaski asked, the slightest trace of a Polish accent in his soft voice. "There should be something. A wooden cross, something."

Walker shook his head. "Kathleen once said that she wanted to be buried under an apple tree in an unmarked grave. She said the purpose of death was to bring new life."

He closed his eyes to hold back the welling tears. Kathleen was so alive in his mind as he remembered the lilt to her voice, the light in her dark eyes, the smile on her lips when she had said: "Each year my friends can come by, pick an apple, take a bite, and say, 'Kathleen is tasting good

this year!' That's the way a person should be remembered—
for life. Not as a pale shell packed away in a silk-lined
box.''

Walker glanced at his white-haired friend, who stood
clutching his Cubs' baseball cap and staring at the flower-
covered grave. "Each year we'll come here," Walker said.
"There will be a small patch of flowers stronger and more
brilliant than those about them. For a brief time we'll know
that Kathleen still lives—see her beauty again."

Janus's head moved from side to side when they turned
from the grave and started back to the stable area. "For me,
I want a marble cross with words chiseled in the stone."

Walker made no reply. Each step took him farther from
the life that had been so clear less than twelve hours ago.
The clear focus he had on his life dissolved into a murky
blur. The disoriented feeling that plagued him after Vietnam
returned. He couldn't shake the sensation he was a disincor-
porated spirit drifting through an alien world.

"Sam, you must come with me into Chicago." Janus's
voice sounded miles distant. "You must tell Paul Nordine
everything that happened last night. The antitoxin is
supposed to kill the Visitors."

Only the dimly lit license plate remained sharply focused
in Walker's mind. 049-ESB, the only thread in his grasp that
led to Kathleen's murderers. He had to follow that thin
strand, had to start pulling it in.

". . . something wrong, terribly wrong." Janus's words
wedged back inside his head. "Paul should know everything. He might have an answer. Sam, you must come with
me."

Walker looked at his elderly friend and nodded. "We'll
go now. I want to talk with this Paul Nordine today."

Janus's head snapped around. "Are you certain?"

"Positive!"

"I can drive you to the stable to get any of your things

you might need." Janus nodded to the dented Pinto parked near the edge of the racetrack. "Then we will head into the city."

"No need to go back to the barn." Walker glanced down at the arsenal he wore. "I've got everything I need."

Janus tugged the stained cap over his snow-white hair and nodded. His pace doubled as he hurried after Walker.

Arlington Heights, Mount Prospect, Des Plaines, one Chicago suburb blended into the next while Janus wheeled the ancient Ford compact down Northwest Highway. All the towns shared one thing—they were empty, abandoned.

Walker shook his head while he watched the streets, houses, and buildings blur by outside. The towns weren't abandoned—their populations had been kidnapped by the Visitors, processed like cattle, and neatly packed away on the great Mother Ships. He could only speculate on the numbers, the millions of men, women, and children still trapped aboard the alien vessels.

In Des Plaines, Janus moved the Pinto up an entrance ramp, through a deserted toll plaza, and south on the Tri-State Tollway. The once bustling, multilane highway appeared as deserted as the Des Plaines Forest Preserve that bordered the eastern side of the road.

Only when they swung east on the Kennedy Expressway near O'Hare International Airport did Walker first glimpse the battle scars Janus mentioned the previous night. No longer did his friend press the gas pedal to the floor. Instead, the former Polish freedom fighter carefully maneuvered the small car through the overturned carcasses of burned-out cars and trucks strewn across the wide lanes of the highway.

Walker grimaced; his head moved sadly from side to side. Janus's description was bad, but he had never expected anything like this. Worse were the charred buildings he saw dotting the area to either side of the expressway.

"Paul Nordine led a raid on the Visitor facilities at O.'Hare about three months ago," Janus said, his blue eyes momentarily leaving the road to glance at his young friend. "This has remained ever since. A reminder from the snakes that resistance was useless. Three hundred men and women died that night. They died fighting rather than being packed away for the lizards to dine on—or hiding like scared rabbits."

Walker ignored the old man's barb. He was alive and they weren't. Who was the real winner? Kathleen's image superimposed itself over the destruction outside the car. He closed his eyes and swallowed, knowing the harsh answer to his question.

Reaching Irving Park, Janus turned off the expressway and drove east. "Would be quicker if we kept to Kennedy— if there was a Kennedy. The road's been blown up between Belmont and Fullerton. Then again between North Avenue and Chicago Avenue. Easier to hit Lake Shore Drive and drop down to the Art Institute."

"The Institute?" Walker lifted an eyebrow. "That's where Visitor Security was."

"Paul liked the idea of sitting up his headquarters there. It shows the people the Visitors are really gone," Janus answered as the Pinto moved over the north branch of the Chicago River.

Walker studied the large areas of destruction they passed. For blocks the city appeared untouched, then there was scorched rubble as though an inferno of incendiary bombs had laid waste to block upon block.

"It's worse here than in other parts of the world," Janus said. "To get at Lake Michigan, the Visitors had to cut us off from everyone else. People could not remain complacent. We saw more, understood quicker. The fighting was hard and long."

Walker nodded. So much had changed during the months he had hidden at the racetrack. Yet, in spite of the ruins, this was better than the empty suburbs. There *were* people here, people building a new life.

When Janus turned right onto Lake Shore Drive, Walker glanced to the west. A smile slid across his lips. Untouched by the hell that had reigned over Chicago, Wrigley Field stood tall and proud. Perhaps it wouldn't be that long before Janus's Cubbies strode onto the playing diamond. The crack of a bat against a ninety-mile-an-hour-plus fastball and cheers of forever hopeful Cubs fans would be a welcome relief after the city's cries of mourning.

"There is the Institute." Janus nodded ahead of them, then glanced at his watch. "Paul should be there by now."

"Good," Walker replied, his thoughts returning to a license plate bearing the number 049-ESB.

Paul Nordine stood inches shorter than Walker's own six feet. The solid muscles packed on his compact frame made him appear even shorter—the body of a plumber rather than a resistance leader. The intelligence reflected in the sharp features of his face and his jet eyes spoke of a mind that grasped more than the ability to join two lengths of pipe together.

After a half hour's wait within the Art Institute, Nordine had called them into his office where he sat with his second-in-command, Steven Tyford, who towered over Nordine by at least six inches. Nordine's handshake was solid and his smile genuine.

Walker also admired his no-nonsense approach. Nordine subtly maneuvered around the polite chitchat, probing directly to the reason for Walker's visit. Then he sat back, listening quietly to the account of the shuttle's rendezvous with the man in the car and Kathleen's murder. Only once did he grab a pen and paper and that was to jot down the license number.

"It can't be, Mr. Walker." Steven Tyford worried a hand through his sandy blonde hair and shook his head when Walker finished. "Only the fifth columnists who aided us on V-Day were given the antitoxin. And I assure you, the snake poison is deadly to the lizards without the antidote."

Nordine's eyes shot to Tyford; the leader shook his head. "Are you certain those in the shuttle were Visitors, Mr. Walk—Sam?"

Walker frowned, uncertain of what Nordine was trying to say. "They were in a Visitor squad vehicle. They wore Visitor uniforms. They carried Visitor rifles. That makes them Visitors in my book."

"Mine too." Nordine nodded.

"But how could they return here?" Tyford shook his head again. "The antitoxin was carefully guarded. They'd have to have it before they could land here."

Nordine nodded again. "Other groups had the antitoxin. The Visitors could have gotten it in another city. Or they could have taken it from our headquarters."

Nordine paused and sucked at his teeth. He then explained the attack on resistance headquarters during the first minutes of the final battle against the Visitors. "There were two plastic pouches of antitoxin there. We assumed they were destroyed when the hotel in Lake Zurich was burned. The truth is the lizards could have cleaned the place out before torching the hotel."

Nordine walked behind a desk cluttered with untidy stacks of papers. He sank into a chair and shook his head. "The fact is the Visitors might easily have gotten their hands on the antitoxin. It could have been here or it could have been in Paris, Cairo, or Hong Kong. Where doesn't matter. What does is to determine if the snakes do indeed have the antitoxin."

"Could those in the shuttle have been some of the fifth columnists Janus told me about?" Walker asked. "It takes a lot for a man to turn against his own kind. I'd think it would be the same for the Visitors."

"A possibility I intend to fully check out, Sam," Nordine answered. "But I think we have to work on the assumption that the snakes do have the antitoxin."

Swiveling his chair about, Nordine handed the paper with the license number on it to Tyford. "Steve, first thing I want you to do is get this to the police and start them working on it. If they can locate the driver of that car, we can find out what the hell he was doing meeting with a Visitor shuttle.

"Then I want you to get fifty volunteers and head back to Arlington Park. If a shuttle landed there once, the Visitors might consider it isolated enough for another landing. I want you there if they decide to come back."

"Nordine, I want to be in that fifty," Walker interrupted.

"I never considered anything else," Nordine replied with a glance at Janus. "I want Janus there too. He knows the area and can put his scroungers on the alert for anything unusual."

Nordine glanced back at Tyford. "Steve, I'm leaving this up to you. I've got my hands full with the Mayor's committee on the upcoming election."

Walker started to protest, then held his tongue. According to Janus, Chicago's power structure had been riddled with Visitor converts—brainwashed humans that were little more than puppets of their alien masters. Nordine and followers had identified the majority of these, many in official positions, had stripped them of power, and placed them under psychiatric care.

While many had taken up the cry to place Nordine in control of the city, the former plumber had steadfastly refused. After meeting the man, Walker could believe Nordine had once said that he had not fought one tyrant just to place another on a throne, even if that tyrant was named Paul Nordine.

"Steve, I want you and your men stationed at the racetrack by this afternoon, understand?" Nordine pushed from his chair and stood. "Now, gentlemen, I'm late for a meeting with the Mayor."

Walker watched Nordine leave the office, then turned to Tyford. The lanky man held out a hand and smiled while Walker accepted his handshake.

"Glad to have you with us, Mr. Walker," he said, then turned to Janus. "It'll take a couple of hours to get the men and the trucks needed to take us out to Arlington Heights. We've set up a commissary in the basement. Not much, but the coffee's hot and we've got sandwiches. I'll meet you there soon as I've got the ball rolling."

"Hot coffee sounds good," Walker answered, trying to remember when he had last tasted anything hot.

As Tyford hastened away to gather his volunteers, Walker and Janus found their way to the basement. Three cups of coffee later, Tyford appeared at the door and waved them to him.

"The men are waiting for us outside. I've got rifles for the both of you," he said. "So unless there's anything else, it's time we went lizard hunting."

Chapter Six

Walker moved away from the row of shrubs in the center field that had concealed him throughout the night. He wiped a hand over his face, then peered at the sky.

To the east, golden pink fingers of light crept above the horizon, heralding sunrise. Westward a line of dark clouds crept across the sky to devour the last purple grays of the predawn morning.

"It will be raining in another hour."

Janus's voice brought Walker around. The old man shuffled through the dew-covered grass, looking as tired and rumpled as Walker felt. He eased a deer rifle from his shoulder and leaned on it when he reached his friend's side.

"Dawn and time for bed." Janus shook his head as they started back to the racetrack's stable area. "One of these days we will live like human beings again instead of night creatures."

Walker only grunted in reply. His mind wandered elsewhere—to the shuttle and its crew of Visitors who had murdered Kathleen. *Where the hell are they?* Out of habit he glanced back at the empty sky. *Maybe they won't be back. Maybe the rendezvous was a fluke—a mistake.*

He clenched his jaw. His knuckles burned white, his grip tightening around the rifle he carried. He couldn't accept that Kathleen's murder had been an accident. Yet for the past week Tyford and his men had kept watch at the abandoned racecourse and the only things they had seen in the sky were a few shooting stars and two jets approaching the reopened O'Hare.

Sucking at his cheeks, Walker shook his head. He had no answers. All he knew was that Kathleen lay buried beneath a carpet of flowers and that the Visitors' squad vehicle had landed to meet a lone man in a dark car. Why the meeting had occurred or if it would happen again were beyond him.

Walker reached the inside rail of the track, ducked under it, crossed the sandy course, and scooted beneath the outside rail. From all parts of the deserted racetrack Tyford's men drifted back to a stable fronting the parking lot that served as headquarters. In their heel-dragging steps, he saw the weary frustration of their fruitless vigil.

Following Janus down the dew-slick embankment, Walker moved across the parking area, swung himself over the low wooden fence, and entered the barn's shedrow. A screen door to one of the tackrooms at the end of the barn was open. Inside, Steven Tyford sat on the edge of his cot, talking into the microphone of a portable radio he had brought with him. Walker half listened but was unable to make out more than a syllable here and there. The man's words droned like the buzz of an annoying insect.

Eventually Tyford hung the microphone on the side of the radio and flicked it off. His shoulders slumped forward, and he sat motionless for several long minutes with his face buried in his hands. When he rose from the cot, his movements held the same weariness Walker had seen in the strides of the men.

"Sam," Tyford said when he reached the tackroom door. There was an embarrassed uneasiness in the lanky man's expression. "I'm afraid I've got some bad news."

Tyford glanced around nervously before his gaze returned to Walker. "I've been talking with Paul Nordine. Things aren't looking good in the city. There're food riots and . . ."

Walker's stomach sank. "And he needs these men," he finished Tyford's sentence.

"He didn't order me to withdraw my men," Tyford replied, worried fingers combing through his shaggy blonde hair. "He said the decision was mine."

"And you've decided to pull out," Walker said, an edge sharpening his words.

Tyford glanced away and nodded. "We've been here a week and seen nothing. I can't justify keeping these men here when they're needed back in Chicago. Sam, I hope you understand. I think that if you were in my—"

Walker pivoted and started from the stable. Paul Nordine's second-in-command had already made up his mind. There was no sense in arguing. It would only waste time.

"Sam!" Tyford called after him. "Sam, where are you going?"

Walker turned to glare at the man. "I'm going to get some sleep. Looks like I'll be by myself tonight."

"Sam, there's no purpose in remaining here," Tyford protested. "We need a man with your skills back in the city. You'll be wasting your—"

"If you don't mind, I'll keep this rifle," Walker cut him off. "I'd like you to leave that radio so I can keep in touch. But I'll understand if you can't."

"Sam, won't you reconsider? There's no purpose—" Tyford started again.

Janus interrupted him this time. "Steven, I intend to remain here with Sam." The old freedom fighter straightened the brim of his ever-present Cubs' cap and stepped to Walker's side.

Together they turned and strolled toward Walker's stall,

leaving Tyford and his men staring after them. By the time they stretched atop the two cots, the heavily laden clouds overhead released their burden. A steady downpour pelted the old barn's roof. With a mumbled curse, Walker tossed onto his side, closed his eyes, and slept.

"They made Hitler's big lie look like a small fib," Janus said, turning to Walker in the darkness. "They infiltrated and conquered with promises of a better world. Mussolini promised to make the trains run on time. Lizard or man—no difference. If we had not struck when we did, we would have seen their blitzkrieg. The same as when Hitler's storm troopers took Poland."

Walker half listened, as he had for the past two hours, to his friend's comparisons of the Visitors' invasion and the insidious beginnings of World War II. He offered no arguments, only muttered an affirmative yes now and then. The Visitors' great leader might have been an alien reincarnation of Adolf Hitler. His tactics were the same; his goals the same.

The only difference between the two, Walker noted, was that the Visitors had implemented their schemes on a global scale. However, he realized, Hitler's conquest might have been worldwide rather than one country at a time had he possessed the Visitors' technology.

"My whole family fought against Hitler when his army swept into Warsaw. Only I survived," Janus continued after a brief pause as they walked outside the shedrow and surveyed the sky. "Only I was left to carry the Brodaski name to the New World."

Even though Janus repeated himself now, Walker listened to his aging friend recount the deaths of his father and mother, his two brothers and sister. Occasionally Walker would leave his station outside his stall and study the sky above.

The rain and the clouds had passed, leaving the heavens clear and the stars diamond bright. A thin sliver of moon had slipped below the western horizon an hour ago, increasing the stars' brilliance. But stars were all Walker saw. The eighth night since Kathleen's murder was halfway gone and still there was no trace of her killers.

"Friends and family, all members of Poland's resistance," Janus said. "I saw them die, Sam. Many drew their last breaths in my arms. The price they paid was dear, but, then, so was the prize they fought for. Freedom—one must be willing to give his life if he wants to keep his freedom."

Walker had believed that once, before Vietnam. In the jungles and rice paddies of Southeast Asia things had jumbled in his head. He fought in his airborne gunboat, but not for anything as lofty as freedom. He fought to survive. To serve out his tour-of-duty and avoid the plastic body bags was all that mattered.

"Some of us never see the danger and hide away like rabbits. Others just take longer to convince that a real danger does exist," Janus continued.

Walker winced. For the first time, one of the old man's barbs sank home. If Janus had seen Vietnam, been there for only one week, he might have understood. However, he hadn't seen a war where the line between the good guys and the bad was so blurred no one was certain it even existed.

"I thought the danger ended after the war," Janus said. "But then there were the Russians. Freedom is a fragile thing. A man must fight all his life."

A dull, vibrating ache suffused Walker's jaw. He went rigid for an instant. Then his arm snaked out, hand closing around the barrel of the rifle that leaned against the stall wall beside him.

"Janus, they're here!"

"Wha—what?" the old man sputtered. He lifted his own rifle. His gaze darted to the night beyond the barn. "Are you certain, Sam? How do you know?"

"I feel them." Walker didn't have time to explain the tricks the Visitors' gravity drive played with his dentalwork. "Come on. Let's move up to the parking lot and see what they're up to."

The two slipped from under the shedrow, took three strides, and froze. Their heads jerked upward. The shuttle they sought silently hovered directly overhead. Its long, white, segmented body drifted down.

Shock made Walker's brain reel. The craft intended to land directly before the stable in which Kathleen and he had hidden for so many months!

"Back!" Walker grabbed Janus's free arm, yanking him into the darkness of the stable's shadows.

Outside the Visitor squad vehicle continued its slow descent. The craft's landing legs were now level with the barn's roof.

"Damn Steven!" Janus's curse hissed through tightly drawn lips. "He should have left the radio!"

"He didn't." Walker's mind raced. They had to reach the resistance in Chicago. Only one way remained for them to accomplish that—Janus's old Pinto. "This way."

Tugging at his friend's arm again, Walker ran down the shedrow, turned left along the wide path encircling the stalls, and darted to the opposite side of the barn. Again he stumbled to a halt.

Not one but *two* of the alien shuttle craft settled to the ground on the opposite side of the barn!

"Son of a bitch!" Walker's gaze darted over his shoulder to see the first ship touch ground.

"Three?" Janus's voice was filled with disbelief. "Why are they landing here?"

Walker didn't have time for speculation. He pointed a finger toward the next barn and urged, "Run! We've got to get out of here before those damned things open up!"

Without hesitation, Janus sprinted forward with Walker at

his heels. His eyes went wide. His fingers released the safety to the deer rifle. Two more of the shuttle vehicles hovered at each end of the barn—five ships in all!

"Subjects are attempting to escape to the west!" a hissing, reptilian voice reverberated from a loudspeaker above.

The floating ship to the right veered its blunt nose and slipped toward the scrambling men. Walker jerked the barrel of his rifle upward, pointed rather than aimed, and squeezed off two shots. The barking reports shattered the night's stillness while tongues of yellow and blue licked at the darkness.

The high-pitched ricochets of two slugs careening off alien metal whined above the echo of the shots. Abruptly the craft swung about again, this time pulling up and banking away from the fleeing men.

Walker took the lead as Janus and he crossed the wide, open strip of land separating the barns. Nor did he stop running once he reached the shedrow of the second structure. Racing around the stable, he shot halfway down the back side, then angled out on a path that would take them to the next barn.

To the east, the sounds of hissing voices shouted orders, demanding that Visitor shock troopers spread out and surround the escaping men. The crunch of stone and sand beneath the soles of urgent boots answered the commands. An image of red-uniformed shock troopers piling from the grounded craft filled Walker's imagination. Each hugged a deadly energy rifle to his chest while his human-disguised face remained hidden beneath a helmet shielded with a black visor.

Reaching the third barn, Walker repeated his ploy and raced on to the fourth. There he halted, hugged the shadows, and gulped down lungfuls of air. "Can't . . . outrun . . . them. Got to . . . to hide. They can . . .

use . . . those damned . . . shuttles like . . . choppers. Keep tabs on us . . . from above . . . while they surround us . . . on the ground."

The dull ache of Walker's jaw told him that was just what the Visitors were doing. Spotlights as powerful as those he had used on his Huey copter in Vietnam sent shafts of blue-white light through the darkness. The ground lay washed in artificial sunlight wherever the beams touched.

"Hide?" Doubt tinged Janus's face and voice. "Where?"

"Here." Walker swung open a stall door and motioned his friend inside.

Janus entered the empty stall, but not without protesting, "All they have to do is open the door to find us."

"Let 'em. We aren't going to be here," Walker said. "We're going to be up there, in the rafters. Unless they've got infrared eyes, they'll never see us."

Taking Janus's rifle and laying it aside, Walker formed a stirrup with his hands to aid his friend in reaching the top of the eight-foot partition that separated the stalls. When Janus safely straddled the wall, Sam passed up the rifles, leaped high, caught the top of the partition, and pulled himself atop the wall. Together they worked into the barn's rafters, climbing toward the pointed ridge of the high roof. Clinging there, they waited, hearts pounding, and rifles aimed below.

Minutes later the shuffle of boots and the muffled mumble of voices came from below. True to Janus's prediction, the shock troopers went straight for the stall doors. Walker's pulse tripled its wild throb as the search moved from one door to another, toward the stall below their precarious perch.

The creak of unoiled hinges came from below. Walker caught his breath; his finger tightened around the trigger of the deer rifle.

A shadow, accompanied by the rustle of hay, moved through the darkness below. The muzzle of Walker's rifle shifted, ready to spit death the instant the alien soldier beneath them lifted his head and gave a cry of discovery. Before Walker died, at least one of the murderers would pay for what they had done to Kathleen.

No shout came. The shadow below turned and walked from the stall. The door closed behind it. Walker's long-held breath escaped in a soft hiss.

"Maybe they do not see as well in the dark as we thought they did," Janus whispered.

Walker said nothing, only eased his finger from the trigger and lifted the muzzle of his rifle. Whether the lizard's poor eyesight or just plain luck protected them he didn't know. That they remained alive—for the moment— was all that mattered. Now all they could do was wait and hope.

Outside the scuffing of booted steps and the reverberating hiss of urgent shouts eventually faded. Walker shifted his position among the rafters to relieve cramping shoulders and arms. Still he waited.

Fifteen minutes after he had heard the last footfall, the dull ache in his molars dissipated. Walker allowed himself a soft sigh of relief. The squad vehicles no longer hovered in the sky above the stable area.

"We'll give it another half hour, then try for your car." He glanced at Janus, who clung to a dusty wooden beam beside him.

"Are you certain they have left?" There was the hint of a quaver in the older man's words.

"I'm not sure of anything except we can't spend the rest of our lives up here." Walker's brow furrowed at the trace of fear he detected in his friend's voice. He shrugged; Janus had a right to be afraid—he knew *he* was.

Head cocking from side to side, Walker strained to hear beyond the natural creaking of the old barn and the night sounds outside. He heard nothing except the soft brush of a gentle night breeze against the roof above.

A million possibilities of what waited outside crowded into Walker's head. He shoved them aside. A Mother Ship might have landed outside in the center field for all he knew, but they couldn't hide here forever. They had to make a try for the car. Nordine and the others had to be warned.

"I'm going down." Walker handed his rifle to Janus. "Wait here until I check things out."

Not giving Janus a chance to answer, Walker slipped from his perch, felt in the darkness with his feet for a rafter, found it, then carefully climbed downward. Reaching the wall partition, he jumped into the musty stall.

He paused and listened. Only night sounds came from outside. The noise of his descent had not brought a scramble of booted feet. Sucking in a steadying breath, he crossed to the stall door and edged it open a crack. Nothing. He pushed the door wider.

The expected blue bolts blazing out of the darkness never came. Only deserted barns stood outside. Walker eased into the shedrow—nothing. A hint of confidence stirring in his pounding heart, he stepped to the outer limits of the barn's shadows and risked a glance at the sky. Blinking stars greeted him.

Gone! Walker's head moved from side to side. It made no sense, but the shock troopers and the shuttles were gone. *Why?* He tried to shuffle the disjointed fragments into place. The five ships had surrounded the barn in which they had waited as though the Visitors had known where they hid. Then the chase through the barns—and the search. Why had the lizards vanished as abruptly as they appeared?

Walker shrugged. He couldn't make head or tail of the situation—only take advantage of it. The way was now clear to Janus's car!

Turning, he trotted back to the stall and threw open the door. "They're gone! Move it!"

Janus dropped the two rifles down to him, then scrambled

from the rafters to the floor of the stall. Alert for a possible trap, the two men moved furtively from their hiding place to the next barn in the long line of stables. The opposite side of the second structure gave no hint of an ambush. With a nod of silent approval they started toward the next barn.

And made it halfway across the open stretch between the two wooden stables before Walker heard the creak of opening stall doors ahead and behind them, then saw the shadows moving within shadows. Shoving Janus to the right, he shouted, "Run! The bastards are all around us!"

Janus stumbled awkwardly for two steps, then broke into long, smooth strides. Walker paced himself so that he remained at the older man's side. To the right and left red-uniformed shock troopers stepped from beneath the barns' shedrows, black rifles clutched in their grip.

"Halt!"

A voice reverberated behind them. Janus ducked his shoulders a bit and hastened his pace with Walker right at his side.

"Halt!" the alien voice demanded again. "There is no escape. Flight is senseless. Throw down your weapons and surrender!"

They've known where we were all along! Walker's brain railed. *They knew before they even landed!*

"Son of a bitch!" Janus's curse growled from his throat.

The reason for his curse—a line of twenty soldiers—ran from both barns to cut off their southern avenue of escape. Both Walker and Janus skidded to a halt. They cast quick glances about them. Shock troopers stood on all four sides with rifles raised.

"Throw down your weapons and surrender," the faceless voice once more commanded. "Do not force us to hurt you."

"The bastards are all around us," Janus hissed through clenched teeth. His eyes rolled toward Walker, questioning.

"We can do two things—surrender or . . ." A metallic click came from Walker's deer rifle as he thumbed off the safety. "Or we can rush them and . . ."

"Take a few with us," Janus finished the sentence, punctuating it with the snap of his own safety. "Rush them!"

The barrel of his rifle jerking around, Janus spun to face the line of helmeted shock troopers in front of the barn to the east. An elongated flower of orange and blue fire blossomed from the barrel of the rifle. Walker's weapon chorused the thunderous voice of his friend's shot. Together they ran head-on toward the waiting soldiers.

"Fire!" A hissing command shouted above the roar of the two rifles.

Walker saw two of the shock troopers ahead stagger backward an instant before blue bolts of crackling energy danced through the night. Two of the globelike discharges struck the center of Janus's chest. A scream ripped from the old man's lips only to be silenced when a third bolt to the back threw him facedown on the ground.

An instant later a white-hot brand of pain seared through Walker's left shoulder. Another slammed into his right thigh. In an agony-maddened dance, he spun about. His finger continuously pumped the rifle's trigger as he blindly sought a target for his fury.

He saw the white-hot bolt. He tried to duck, to dodge. He couldn't. Fire exploded across his chest. He screamed as pain washed through every cell of his body. Then darkness rushed at him. Gratefully, he sank into the outstretched arms of oblivion.

Chapter Seven

The aching throb of his teeth drew Walker up the pitch-black well shaft toward the humming above him. He moaned, and his eyes cautiously blinked open, expecting a harsh deluge of stabbing light. Dimness greeted him, a diffused dusklike light.

And the hum? It was neither above nor below. It surrounded him in a barely perceivable envelope. It was a noise he might have ignored were it not for the damnable throb pulsing at the root of each tooth in his mouth.

He lifted a hand to massage his jaw. His fingers shakily crept up three inches before he moaned again. Every muscle in his body ached. He felt as though a steamroller had driven across him while he . . .

While I . . . while I did what? He blinked, then groaned as an invisible vise clamped about his neck when he attempted to shake his head. *What's happened to me? Where am . . .*

Walker's eyes flew wide to stare wildly into the dimness. *A squad vehicle!* It came rushing at him like a tidal wave—

the five shuttles, the shock troopers, the burning bolts from the energy rifles. *I'm aboard a Visitor shuttle!*

It made no sense, but he was alive. He remembered the blasts to his shoulder and leg. Then came the sizzling cascade of blue that seared into his chest. He had been struck by three charges from the lizards' rifles, yet he still lived!

Gritting his teeth to fight past the stiffness cording his muscles, he gingerly probed at his chest. His brow furrowed. There was no cauterized flesh burnt to a crisp by the bolt. Even his black turtleneck remained in one piece. Only a fine soot and the odor of scorched fabric marked where the blast had struck.

Walker's eyes rolled to the side, then to his thigh. Except for the soreness, there was no indication he had been hit. He ignored the painful twinges awakened by his movement and pushed to his elbows. Drawing up the bottom of his shirt, he stared at an angry-looking red circle at the center of his chest.

"It looks like a bad sunburn. Feels like one too."

Walker's head jerked around. Janus sat against a wall with his arms hugging his knees. "The snakes had their rifles on stun. They never meant to kill, only capture."

"Capture us?" With a miminum of groans and curses, Walker managed to sit and scoot around to face his friend. "Why would they want to take us prisoner?"

Janus snorted with contempt. "They are having us for dinner. Why else?"

"You're too old and stringy to be anybody's main course." Walker tried to make light of the old man's remark.

Neither Janus nor he smiled. In truth, he could think of no other reason to explain their capture. Rumors maintained that the Visitors preferred their meat freshly killed—or still living.

"Well, I plan to give a few of the scaly bastards a case of permanent indigestion before they serve me up on a platter," Walker said as he started to rise.

"Don't stand—"

Walker pushed to his feet. The back of his head rammed into a solid, unyielding ceiling.

"—up!" Janus's warning came a fraction of a second too late.

Walker crumpled back to his knees, cursing. His gaze shot about him. The dimness was deceptive. They weren't in a room, as he had first thought, but within what now appeared to be some type of storage compartment with a ceiling no more than four feet high.

"Why in hell didn't you warn me?" He glared at Janus. "I could have taken off the top of my skull."

"I did." Janus shrugged. "You were too worried about snake indigestion to listen."

"If I were you, I'd be worried too." Walker peered about him. The compartment was seamless. If there was an exit, he couldn't find it. "Unless we find a way out of here before they take off, neither one of us will be able to avoid that dinner."

On his knees, Walker worked his way around the six-foot-deep and five-foot-wide compartment. His fingertips confirmed what his eyes perceived. The walls and the ceiling were without seams. It was as though they had been poured and molded as a single piece of metal—or plastic. Walker was unable to distinguish the alien material.

"Son of a bitch!" He hammered a fist against a wall in frustration. "How in hell are we supposed to get out of here if we can't find a door?"

"I do not think the snakes intend for us to get out of here until they're ready for us." Janus shifted to his knees and made a circuit of the cubicle. "Warm or cool?" he asked when he reached the younger man's side.

"Warm or cool?" Janus repeated. He nodded toward the wall nearest them. "This is warmer than that wall. Which way do you think is out?"

"If the Visitors are true reptiles, the cold would make them sluggish," Walker answered. "I'd say the interior of the ship is behind the warm wall."

"So would I if it were not for that news report that made all the networks shortly after the Mother Ships appeared," Janus said as he shifted to face the cooler wall. "Remember? The one about a Visitor saving a chemical plant worker in a vat of liquid nitrogen or oxygen or something?"

Walker frowned, then nodded vaguely, recalling the incident. Since the alien spacecraft had first arrived, the news had been primarily devoted to the Sirians. It was hard to remember them all, or to distinguish the truth from the overwhelming lies that had deceived a whole planet.

Janus leaned back on his elbows, lifted his legs, and placed the soles of his shoes flat against the cooler wall. "Here goes nothing."

His legs jerked back, then shot forward to slam against the wall. He cursed, then kicked at the wall again. On Janus's third attempt, Walker's legs lashed out with him, and the younger man's curses echoed those of his friend. Each thrust of his feet sent fresh waves of pain through his sore body.

"No good," Janus panted after several minutes and collapsed to his back.

Even in the dim light, Walker saw the agony his friend tried to conceal. He felt the painful protests of his own body. He could only imagine the torture of a man nearly twice his age. Yet they had to try to escape. They had to!

"Rest a bit, and we'll give it another go," Walker said, slamming his feet out at the wall one last time.

His legs shot straight out into empty air, knee joints popping loudly. His boot soles met no resistance.

Walker jerked up. The wall was gone and he was staring straight into the dark muzzle of an energy rifle!

"Out!" a female voice ordered from behind the weapon. The rifle jerked to the side, motioning them from the storage compartment. "Both of you crawl out nice and easy. No funny business. I'd hate to lose you after getting you this far."

This far? What the hell does she mean? Walker's gaze scanned the chamber outside his prison. The diffused light was slightly brighter beyond the compartment. In it stood at least twenty pairs of shiny black shock trooper boots. The muzzles of an equal number of rifles provided an irrefutable argument against trying any "funny business."

On hands and knees he crawled into the chamber with Janus right behind him. The muzzle of the rifle nodded upward. Without question, he followed the motion and stood. A sinking sensation sent his stomach plummeting. He had underestimated the soldiers lining the chamber. A minimum of fifty uniformed aliens packed the vessel's interior.

"Lock your hands behind your heads and slowly back against the wall." The reverberating female voice sounded behind the helmet's faceplate again while the muzzle of the trooper's rifle centered on Walker's chest.

Shrugging helplessly, he complied, as did Janus. A soft hiss drew Walker's attention to the side. The door to the storage compartment lay closed, once more indiscernible from the craft's wall.

"Ah, our guests have awakened." A male voice came from the left. "I was afraid we would have to carry them into the Mother Ship. Alicia would have been irritated at having to wait for them to regain consciousness."

The shock troopers pressed back toward the ship's walls, opening a narrow path through their ranks. For an instant Walker glimpsed the blinking lights of what appeared to be a U-shaped control console at the far end of the shuttle. Above the multihued array stretched a wide window. He caught his breath. Beyond that loomed a monstrous oblate spheroid—a Visitor Mother Ship!

God! We're in space! Walker's stomach dropped another twenty stories with the realization of his total helplessness. How could there be escape here? *Hell, I don't even know where here is!*

A man rose from one of the two chairs at the control console and walked toward the rear of the squad vehicle. He lifted a helmet from his head. Janus gasped.

"Friend Janus, we meet again." The Visitor pushed a stray strand of blonde hair from his forehead and smiled at the older captive.

"Gerald?" Janus's head moved from side to side in disbelief. "You were killed with ten other fifth columnists at Daley Center on V-Day!"

Gerald chuckled, a wide grin moving across his face. "As you can see I'm very much alive. Another took my place in the city. A necessary ruse, since I led the attack on your resistance headquarters that day. You should have been there, Janus. It would have saved you this little trip."

"A spy!" Janus spat. "Son of a bitch!"

Gerald laughed. "You confuse me with the offspring of a mammal. The comparison leaves something to be desired."

Walker only half heard the exchange. His gaze focused on the gargantuan craft outside. A rectangular opening appeared amid the rows of lights illuminating the Mother Ship's curved hull. The shuttle nosed toward the gaping mouth of glaring light.

Inside he saw a scurry of movement over what appeared to be a landing deck. Red-uniformed Visitors darted here and there among line upon line of squad vehicles. Walker could only guess at what force the aliens employed to prevent those within the landing bay area from being sucked out of the open port into the vacuum of space.

Without another trajectory correction, the shuttle shot within the illuminated port and hovered above a red bull's-eye painted on the white deck. Gently the craft settled atop the concentric circles with no more of a jar than a halting elevator.

"The antitoxin at headquarters—you and these other snakes took it! That is why you are not dead!" Janus was saying when Walker turned back to the tall, young-looking Visitor called Gerald.

The blonde, disguised alien only grinned and nodded to the doors that opened in the side of the shuttle. "I wish we could continue this conversation, Janus, but there is someone waiting to talk with you two. It's considered dangerous to keep Alicia waiting."

The barrel of an energy rifle nudged Walker's ribs. Hands still locked behind the back of his head, he turned and walked from the shuttle. He stumbled awkwardly when his feet touched the white landing deck, shocked by the vastness surrounding him.

Kilometers rather than mere meters leaped to mind while his eyes attempted to soak in the immensity of the landing bay. It stretched endlessly to his right and left. The ceiling itself rose at least three stories above his head. And the number of shuttles standing at attention atop the white deck? He couldn't even hazard a guess.

"Through the corridor ahead." Gerald nodded to an oddly shaped tunnel that opened across the bay directly before Walker. He pointed to two shock troopers who took the lead. Another six boxed in the two prisoners as they moved toward the corridor.

The light dimmed when they entered the angular walkway. Walker blinked, gave his eyes time to accustom themselves to the dusklike glow, then scanned smooth walls, floor, and ceiling.

The alien characters neatly stenciled here and there with red arrows pointing their directions provided him no clue to his location. Instead, he tried to memorize the twists and turns his lizard guard made at each tunnel junction. After ten minutes he gave up.

Even if he managed to escape Gerald and the shock troopers, Walker realized he would be lost in this maze of corridors in a matter of seconds. And if—*just if*—he found his way back to the shuttle bay, what then? He was a chopper pilot, not an astronaut. How could he expect to fly an unfamiliar craft through space back to Earth? There was more to space flight than just pointing the nose of a craft at your destination and putting the pedal to the floor.

Turning to the left at the next tunnel junction, the guards ahead entered a large chamber. They halted before a black-outlined door at the far end of the immense room. Gerald stepped to the door and placed his hand on a green-glowing square inset in the wall. The door slid back.

Again the vastness of the Visitors' Mother Ship sent Walker's mind spinning. The room on the opposite side of the door was three times the size of the chamber they had exited. Instead of smooth, featureless walls, panels of blinking lights ran from floor to ceiling like some Hollywood set designer's vision of a futuristic computer.

At the opposite end of the room stretched a far less gaudy appearing control console. Five white-smocked Visitors sat in chairs before the wide console, flicking switches and staring up at a glass-enclosed chamber beyond their position. The center chair swiveled about to reveal an extraordinarily beautiful woman. With a toss of her shoulder-length blonde hair, she stared at the newcomers.

Perhaps too beautiful, Walker thought while he studied the woman, unable to shake the sensation that there was something wrong, something out of place about the human-disguised blonde. Search as he did, he couldn't put his finger on the flaw, nor could he quiet the nagging at the back of his mind.

"Bring them closer, Gerald." Her blue eyes narrowed as she spoke.

"Yes, Alicia." Gerald prodded Walker and Janus forward, stopping them a yard from the seated commander of the Mother Ship.

Alicia's gaze slowly moved over Walker and then to Janus. She drew a deep breath and shook her head. "These are the two our contact spoke of? Somehow I expected more."

"They will serve us well, rest assured of that. This one is trusted within the resistance movement." Gerald anxiously pointed to Janus. "And this is the one whose woman we killed. No one in Chicago will even suspect either of being a convert."

"Convert!" Janus went rigid. His eyes glared at Gerald, then Alicia. "Never! Janus Brodaski will never serve snakes! I will die before I let you control my mind!"

Alicia chuckled dryly, without a trace of humor. "Perhaps you will. A few have lacked the strength to endure conversion. However, far more have lived to serve Our Great Leader and his cause. I think you will be among the latter."

Abruptly Alicia swiveled her chair back to the control console. "We waste time, Gerald. Strip them and place them in the conversion chamber. I've other duties to attend to."

Eight energy rifles rose, their barrels homing in on the two human captives. Gerald glanced at Janus and Walker. "Remove your clothing."

"No." Walker forced all the strength he possessed into that single word. Open confrontation, if only verbally, was the last tactic remaining to him. "Go ahead and have your goons pull their triggers. Two dead men will be of no use to you."

Janus sucked at his cheeks and spat directly into Gerald's face. "Better to die than be lizard zombies!"

The cool gleam of Gerald's blue eyes dropped 50 degrees as he wiped the spittle away. His hand then lashed out and grasped Janus's left wrist. The Visitor jerked the old man's arm out straight, squeezing until the fingers of Janus's hand splayed wide.

"If it's death you wish, it can be arranged." Gerald's gaze shifted to Walker while unholstering a pistol strapped at his waist. "But I assure you it will not be a quick, clean death."

As Walker stared on, Gerald placed the muzzle of his weapon atop the lower joint of Janus's little finger. A faint click sounded. A blue bolt of energy sizzled.

Janus screamed. His body shuddered, knees folding beneath him. Two guards grasped him under the armpits to hold his trembling form upright.

Walker's eyes went wide, shifting between his friend's deathly pale face and the blackened tip of his small finger—a finger that was now short one joint. The sickening smell of burned flesh invaded the younger man's nostrils.

"The human mind and body can endure an extraordinary amount of agony before it finally accepts the inevitability of death. There are means to extend both the time and the pain required before that decision is reached." Gerald moved the pistol to the next knuckle of Janus's finger. He fired a second time.

"Nooooo!" Walker's scream mingled with his friend's blood-chilling cry.

He lurched forward, arms outstretched for Gerald's throat. Before he covered an inch, two guards grabbed him from behind. Like unbreakable bands of steel, those arms encircled him, holding him immobile.

"Please . . . please . . ." Janus panted, his pain-contorted face drenched in sweat.

Gerald edged the muzzle of his pistol to the last joint of the finger. "The decision isn't mine, Janus, but is with your stubborn friend."

"Sam." Janus's eyes rolled to Walker. "It hurts . . . please. It hurts so badly."

The unconquerable Janus Brodaski Walker had come to know during his months of hiding was gone. An old man stood in his stead—an old man suffering as his little finger was burned away joint by joint. Hate filled Walker's dark eyes when they turned to Gerald again.

The Visitor merely shrugged and pulled the pistol's trigger once again.

"No more!" Walker shouted, trying to drown out Janus's scream of agony. "No more. I'll do what you want."

A pleased smile lifted the corners of Gerald's mouth. He nodded to the guards. "Strip them and put them into the chamber."

Rough, cold hands yanked the turtleneck over Walker's head, then skinned away his boots and pants. Gooseflesh covered his body as the ship's cool air bathed his nakedness. A stray thought pushed into his head—the temperature was too cold for true reptiles—at least terrestrial reptiles.

"Sam . . ."

Janus looked at Walker, his lips trembling as though unable to find the words he wanted to say. His eyes then sadly rolled to the floor, his head sagging on his shoulders as four guards led him toward the glass-enclosed chamber. Before Walker could assure his friend that he understood, his own guards shoved him forward.

Two glowing circles of light appeared on—no, within!—the floor of the conversion cage. The guards positioned

Janus at the center of the farthest, then Walker atop the other. The moment the lizards' grip loosened, Walker lunged toward the glass plate behind which the Mother Ship's commander sat at the control console. Or tried to lunge. The muscles of his legs and arms refused to move.

"Struggle is useless." Alicia's voice floated through the chamber. "*I* now control your body."

Walker stared while the woman-masked alien pressed a glowing yellow button before her. In spite of the commands his brain screamed to the contrary, his right arm, then his left, lifted and stretched toward Alicia.

"When you willingly offer me this embrace, you will be mine." Alicia's voice surrounded Walker, pressed inward, and penetrated his skull. She spoke within his mind now. "And you *will* embrace me with tears of joy, Samuel Walker. I promise you that."

"Never!" Walker defiantly spat his denial of that promise.

It was a statement that would have boosted his confidence had he been certain that he actually spoke the words. He heard himself, or thought he heard himself, but his lips did not move. He tried to clamp his eyes closed; they remained open.

"You will embrace me, Sam. Together we shall share untold pleasures—pleasures undreamed of by man." The hissing reverberation of Alicia's voice faded, leaving a lilting invitation of seduction.

Beyond the barrier of glass, Alicia pushed from her chair. A knowing smile moved over her red lips. She stepped atop the console with its rows of glowing buttons and switches. With a shrug of her shoulders, the white lab smock she wore fell away. Her arms reached out, and she stepped through the solid wall of glass into the chamber.

No. It can't be! Walker's brain struggled to reject the matter-defying creature who filled his vision.

"Embrace me, Sam. Take me into your arms and love me. Love me, and I will protect you. Love me, and I will see that no harm comes to you or your friend."

Even as she spoke, Alicia's red uniform melted from her body. She stood before him unashamed of her nakedness, delighting as his eyes roved over the firm, high, upthrusted cones of her breasts, the coral-blushed pinkness of her nipples, down the flatness of her stomach to the sensual well of her navel, down to the . . .

"NO!" Walker's head jerked from side to side. And it *did* wrench from left to right—he felt it! His eyes rose back to the opulent mounds of her breasts. Before he had the nagging sensation that something was wrong with Alicia. Now he understood. "Lizards don't have breasts! Fake! You're a fake—a snake!"

The alluring invitation in Alicia's eyes fired to flaming rage. Like hot wax running down a candle, her human disguise melted, dripping away to reveal a face of green scales mottled with patches of black. Slitted eyes of orange and yellow glared where orbs of aquamarine had beckoned him but moments ago. An angry red forked tongue flicked from her mouth.

"Snake!" Walker spat into her hissing face. *"Snake!"*

"Very well, Samuel Walker, if you won't embrace me . . ." Alicia faded from within the chamber. In a heartbeat she sat at the control console dressed in her stiff red uniform, the beauty of her human-disguised face returned. ". . . then embrace yourself!"

Walker's outstretched arms curled inward to hug himself tightly. *Illusion*. He recognized Alicia's nude image for what it had been, told himself the control she held over his arms was the same. But he *felt* his fingers and palms grasping the flesh of his arms and sides.

"Embrace your whole self!" Alicia's voice hissed at the center of his skull.

A maelstrom of light exploded around him. Spinning, swirling, churning, it swept away the conversion chamber, the control room outside. Time and space reached out, clasped him in invisible fingers, and sent him hurling head-on to . . .

The Huey's controls went dead in his hands. Joystick and pedals brought no response. Overhead the helicopter's rotory blades sang wildly out of control. The ship dipped, then plunged into the ocean of jungle below.

Illusion! Walker's brain railed.

"No illusion, Yankee! You die now."

Walker stood tied to the trunk of a tree. The odors of the rain forest mixed with the smell of fear in his nostrils. An ancient Vietnamese smiled at him from beneath a straw hat. Behind the gray-bearded man in the black pajamas burned the flaming wreckage of his chopper.

"Die now," the old man repeated as he pulled Walker's bayonet from its sheath. With both hands he jerked the silvery blade high above his head, then drove downward toward Walker's vulnerable chest.

Illusion! Walker defied the blade that drove hilt deep into his flesh. *Illusion! Damn you, Alicia! Damn all you lizards!*

Nothing.

Walker floated in—nothing. Total and complete nothingness caressed him. No sound, not even in the racing pound of his heart. No color: his transparent skin revealed a transparent skeleton and transparent organs. Nothingness.

Alone. Walker felt but did not feel cold sweat prickle over his nonbody. The blurred focus, the disorientation, the loneliness he had felt all those years after the war swallowed him. He floated, lost and alone.

Illusion! he realized again.

"You fear the loneliness, Sam." He heard but didn't hear Alicia's words. "Lost—forever! Alone for eternity! Will you drift in nothingness until time ends, or will you embrace me?"

"Illusion!" Walker forced himself to scream to the featureless void.

The nothingness remained. Walker whimpered. *No. No. No.*

"Reach out and embrace me," Alicia whispered. "All you have to do is take me into your arms."

Walker retreated. The lizard bitch played within his mind. She probed, searching his fears, seeking the key to break him. Life had tried the same thing and failed. Kathleen had saved him from the loneliness. Kathleen had brought back the clear focus.

Kathleen, he called to his memories. Within the nothingness, he molded her image. Lovingly she smiled and called to him. *Kathleen*. He went to her, arms open.

"No!" Alicia's voice hissed. "She is dead!"

Kathleen dissipated. In her place stood grinning Death, skeletal arms outstretched to receive Walker. He ran, scurrying back into the nothingness, back into the loneliness.

"Only I can save you from yourself, Sam." Alicia was there again. Her voice was like a gentle spring breeze. "Embrace me. Accept me. That is all I ask. Embrace me and we will be together forever."

"Noooo!" Walker's nonvoice rebounded off the nothingness and folded back over him. He screamed and screamed and screamed. No one heard, no one answered. Only the eternal void watched.

Chapter Eight

Walker felt cold hands pull him screaming from the nothingness. Lights, blurred and tumbling, hue-shifting lights cartwheeled through the fuzzy cotton packed over his eyes while the hands jerked and tugged at him. He blinked. The cotton dissipated, a helmeted head winked into shape, then the cotton returned.

"The . . . the . . . session . . . session . . . went . . . went . . . well . . . well?" Gerald's voice echoed somewhere in the distance.

"Well . . . well . . . as . . . as . . . can . . . can . . . be . . . be . . . expected . . . expected . . . for . . . for . . . the . . . the . . . first . . . first . . . time . . . time . . . in . . . in . . . the . . . the . . . chamber . . . chamber." Alicia's reverberating answer sounded just as distant.

Two pairs of arms grasped Walker under the armpits and dragged him forward. A punch-drunk smile slid across Walker's face. Alicia's voice was as far away as Gerald's! She no longer lived in his head! The nothingness was gone!

Gone! His smile widened to a silly grin. *And I'm still*

Samuel Walker—human being. Human being, you damned lizard bitch! Human being!

"There's no need to help me. I can walk." A weak wiggle of his head was the best he could manage against the arms hauling him forward. He tried to get his feet under him, but only stubbed a toe. "Then again, I might need a tad bit of assistance."

His head turned from side to side. Two helmeted heads were visible through the fog of cotton. Ahead lay a blur of corridors, the ever-twisting and turning maze of tunnels that ran through the Visitors' Mother Ship. How bright the strangely diffused light appeared after the nothingness!

He heard a mechanical hiss, saw a rush of white, and in the next moment was dumped facedown on a pillowless cot. The retreating footsteps of his two strong-armed escorts disappeared when the hiss sounded again.

"Sam?"

Walker pushed to his elbows, forced his head up, and focused until the cotton parted to reveal Janus seated on a cot three feet from him. Turning his head from side to side, Walker sent his gaze about the tiny cell in which he had been placed. Except for a narrow aisle running between them, the two cots completely filled the compartment.

"Sam?" Janus asked again. "Are you all right, Sam?"

Walker managed a weary nod. "Still human."

"Then sit up," Janus demanded.

"What?" Walker's eyes rolled up to his friend.

"I said sit up, Sam." Janus's voice was urgent. "Right now, sit up."

With a groan of protest, Walker rolled to a side, balanced there for a shaky moment, then pushed upright. He sat with his back against a cool wall, staring at the old man. "I don't know what you want, but this better be good. You have no idea what it took just to . . ."

"Catch!" Janus tossed a shoe at his friend.

Without thought, Walker's right hand leaped up and snagged the shoe. "What in hell was that about?"

"Making certain you *are* still human." Janus smiled weakly. "Visitor converts were first spotted by their hands. A right-handed man entered the chamber and came out a left-handed convert."

"And I'm still right-handed. Hmm." Walker smiled. He studied the shoe clenched in his right hand.

Abruptly he flung the shoe across the cell directly at Janus. The old man's right hand jerked up and caught it. Walker's smile grew.

"Do not be so smug." Janus lifted his left hand from his lap and held it so Walker could see the blackened stump that once had been a finger. "Not even a snake could catch anything with a hand in this shape."

Deep furrows etched across Walker's brow. While he had floated in the nothingness of Alicia's conversion chamber, he forgot about Gerald working Janus over with his pistol. Walker moved to the edge of the cot. "How is it?"

Janus waved him away and nodded at a black bundle lying at the foot of his friend's cot. "Put your clothes on before you freeze. The damned snakes have got it too cold in here."

Before he began to dress, Walker lifted a blanket from the bottom of Janus's cot and covered the old man. As painful as the hand might be, Walker discerned no sign of infection about the wound. Gerald's energy bolts had cauterized the raw flesh when they sheared the finger away.

"How long do you think it will be before we are both using our left hands instead of the right ones?" Janus asked while Walker tugged on trousers and socks.

"We'll be out of here before that." Walker tried to sound confident when the one thing he now lacked was confidence.

"It will not be long with me, Sam." Janus's voice went

deep and sober. "It was rough in there today. She read my mind like a book—flipped through the pages until she found the buttons she needed. Then it all came alive again, Sam. My family, my friends, all of them were there. So were the Nazis. She made me live it again. Made me . . ."

His voice trailed away, and he sat staring at his left hand. Walker closed his eyes and drew a deep breath to steady himself before he stretched out on the cot. Janus was right. Although Walker had no idea how the conversion chamber worked, today Alicia had merely used it to read them, to find the weaknesses and fears needed to remold their minds.

"She had us in there most of the day, Janus," Walker answered. "She couldn't break us. She won't be able to break us."

"We were in the chamber less than an hour." Janus lifted his right arm to expose the face of a wristwatch. "Less than an hour."

Again Walker closed his eyes and sucked in a deep breath. *Less than an hour.* He had floated in that soulless nothingness for an eternity before the shock troopers had pulled him free.

Opening his eyes, he gazed around the tiny cell. Nothing had changed since his first fuzzy glance. At the foot of the cots stood a solid-looking door. On the ceiling was a narrow grating covering an air duct perhaps six inches wide. The light was dim, the same sourceless, diffused illumination he had seen throughout the Mother Ship. The only way in and out was the door.

"Janus, did you notice anything when they brought you in here?" Walker asked. "Anything that might help us get out of here."

Janus didn't answer. Walker turned. The old man lay snuggled beneath the blanket, eyes closed, and mouth open in a soft snore. Exhaustion, mental and physical, had taken its toll. For a moment Walker considered reaching out and shaking his friend awake, then pushed the thought away.

Instead, Walker closed his own eyes. Janus was also right about the time it would take before they both were nice, obedient Visitor converts. A session or two more in the chamber and Walker would gladly reach out and embrace Alicia. Before that he had to find a way to escape, even if they died in the attempt! And before that he needed rest.

He rolled onto his side and drifted to sleep within seconds only to find his dreams haunted by visions of a Death-faced Kathleen.

The mechanical hissing of the opening cell door brought Walker straight up on the cot. A helmeted shock trooper with rifle in hand stood in the doorway.

"Wake your friend, Mr. Walker. We haven't much time if we are to get you out of here before Alicia comes calling again." The voice behind the smoky faceplate was female, the same one that had ordered them from the shuttle's cargo compartment. "Please hurry. There really isn't much time."

"Wha—what is it?" Janus blinked awake and sleepily glanced at the armed Visitor, then at Walker. "What is going on, Sam?"

"Your guess is as—"

"There isn't time to explain everything now," the shock trooper interrupted. The helmet's faceplate flipped up to reveal a very beautiful and very feminine face. Strands of soft brunette hair poked out beneath the helmet to frame the worry lines that tautened the woman's oval face. "Please hurry. Strip these two guards and get into their uniforms!"

For the first time Walker noticed the two forms crumpled outside the door. His eyes shot back to the guard who had escorted them from the shuttle. He shook his head with determination. "We don't move a muscle until we know what's happening."

"Damn you stubborn humans!" Exasperation tightened the woman's voice. Her eyes darted to the open door. "Someone might come along at any moment and discover these two!"

"Not a muscle," Walker reaffirmed his stubbornness. "We've had one taste of your Commander Alicia's toys. We aren't about to run head-on into something she's dreamed up to make our stay more interesting."

"Alicia has nothing to do with this. My name is Jennifer. I'm with the fifth columnists aboard this Mother Ship. If you'll get off your backsides and move, there's a chance, just a chance, I might be able to save your lives." Both her voice and green eyes pleaded with him.

Still neither Walker nor Janus moved.

"Fools! You're scheduled for another session in the conversion chamber in six hours. In two hours a supply shuttle for the Arlington Heights outpost will leave from bay one," Jennifer continued. "We barely have time to make that shuttle. Even then I can't guarantee Alicia won't discover your escape before we land. Now, will you two please hurry?"

Janus glanced at Walker, who nodded. The two men pushed from their cots and dragged the guards into the cell. Dead or unconscious, Walker didn't waste time to check either of the soldiers. Instead, he helped Janus strip his man, then turned his attention to his own guard. Minutes later the two stood disguised in red uniforms and helmets. Both lifted energy rifles and pointed them at Jennifer.

"We are going with you, but do not think we trust you," Janus said.

"At the first sign of a trap, I can guarantee there will be at least one char-broiled lizard," Walker added, leaving no doubt as to his intentions.

Jennifer's green eyes rolled to the ceiling. She gritted her teeth with disgust. "Then I suggest you learn to use the rifles. There's a knob on the side to adjust power settings. Full forward is kill. Both of yours are presently on stun. The lever beneath the knob is a primer. Now can we leave?"

Flicking the knob full forward, Walker nodded for the woman to lead the way. Jennifer closed the cell behind them, then started down a corridor on the left. Five right-angle turns later, she halted beside a hatch. Her fingers danced over a panel containing ten buttons inset on the wall. The hatchway hissed open.

"It's a maintenance shaft. It'll be safer than keeping to the main corridors." Jennifer waved them inside. "At least for a while."

"Why not just walk straight into the shuttle?" Walker asked when the door closed behind them. "No one's going to recognize us in these uniforms."

"Listen to yourself and you'll know the reason." Jennifer shook her head. "One word from either of you and every shock trooper on board would be down on us. We'll stick to my route, if you don't mind."

Jennifer pivoted. Before he could answer, she strode down the cramped shaft, signaling them to follow. Walker tightened his grip on the rifle and stepped after her with the muzzle aimed directly at the small of the woman's back. He couldn't be certain, but it seemed to him that she was now leading them back the way they came.

Five more angular turns in the shaft and three junctions later, Walker had completely lost any sense of direction. He simply moved down the shaft lined with pipes and wire, with Jennifer ahead and Janus behind. For all he could tell, the woman was taking them around in circles.

He sucked at his teeth. To free them from the cell, provide hope of escape, and then recapture them just before they reached the shuttle would be the type of trick Alicia would enjoy. What perfect subjects for conversion they would make—bone weary from their flight and with spirits broken.

"Up." Jennifer stopped beside a ladder set in the wall of the maintenance shaft. "We've got to climb to the next level."

Walker's neck craned back. A dark, narrow tunnel opened in the ceiling of the shaft. The ladder's rungs ran up for a hundred feet. Dim light came from the top of the tunnel. He looked at Jennifer. "After you."

With a shrug, she started up the ladder. Walker turned to Janus. The young man looked questioningly at his friend's left hand.

Janus peered at the overhead shaft, drew a heavy breath, released it, and nodded. "I can make it."

Walker stepped aside to let him follow the woman. Just in case the old man couldn't make it on his own, Walker would be below to lend a helping shoulder. Slinging the rifle over a shoulder, he grasped a rung over his head and began to climb.

Halfway up the tunnel Janus's grunts and curses kept Walker's attention riveted above. Now and then he caught a glimpse of the pained grimace that masked the old man's face each time he placed pressure on his mutilated left hand. However, Janus did not quit. Sweat glistening from his pale face, his breath wheezing in sharp gasps, the former Polish freedom fighter crawled from the tunnel at Jennifer's heels.

"It's easier from here on," Jennifer reassured Janus while she helped him stand. "We'll have to go down to the lower level again, but there'll be no climbing."

Walker pushed from the narrow shaft and stood. They were at a wide junction of four maintenance tunnels. His right eyebrow arched dubiously when he looked at Jennifer. Her own gaze momentarily dropped to the rifle muzzle still aimed at her.

"There's an exit ahead," she said, starting down the shaft to her right. "We have to travel a main corridor for about two hundred of your meters, then we cut through a storage area before moving down to bay one."

True to her description, the fifth columnist stopped beside a hatch fifty yards down the shaft. Again her finger danced over a panel of buttons. The door slid open and a rush of cool air bathed Walker's face.

"Why is it colder here?" Walker exited the hatchway.

"Quiet!" Jennifer warned by placing a finger to her lips. "This portion of the ship isn't frequented, but there are guards. You can't let them hear you speak."

"The cold?" Walker insisted in a low whisper.

Irritation flashed in Jennifer's green eyes. "All the compartments in this section are for storage. The temperature has been lowered to . . ."

She hesitated. Her gaze moved nervously between her two human companions. "It's easier to show you than explain. This way. And drop your faceplates. I don't want any guards glimpsing your faces."

Walker cursed to himself as he stumbled after the woman. The faceplate's smoky coloring transformed the corridor's dim lighting to night. If Jennifer were leading them into a trap, now was the perfect time to spring it. He was virtually blind.

A hundred meters down the corridor the need for the faceplates became evident. Two shock troopers stepped from an opening door. Their heads twisted toward the approaching threesome.

"Is there anything wrong, Sergeant?" the nearest of the soldiers asked.

"Spot inspection," Jennifer answered, her tone military and crisp. "Carry on with your duties."

The two saluted, waited for Walker to pass, then turned and marched off down the corridor in the direction the trio had come. Walker's finger eased from the rifle's trigger as he released his breath.

When Jennifer stopped again, it was in front of a wide hatch. Carefully this time, her fingers punched out a code on the panel of buttons on the wall beside the door. The hatch opened with a hiss like that of an escaping breath, a sound that matched Walker's own gasp.

"Now you understand the cold," Jennifer said when they entered the area beyond.

Walker edged his faceplate back and stared about him. He understood only too well. "This is the storage room you mentioned?"

Jennifer nodded. Her eyes lowered in shame.

"You slimy snakes." Janus pushed back his helmet's faceplate. All the color drained from his face while his gaze traveled about him. "You bastards. Even Hitler's ovens could not equal this."

Room or compartment did not describe the area. Canyon came closer to it. They stood on a wide catwalk that stretched for what appeared to be miles ahead of them. Walker stepped to the railing and peered down. His head went dizzy. It was like gazing at the ground from atop the Sears Tower. The alien-constructed canyon rose just as high above them.

Packing this immense, yawning chamber were row upon row of neatly stacked clear capsules. A milky gelatinous substance filled each of the capsules. But that wasn't what churned Walker's stomach—it was the shadowy but discernible human forms that floated within the gelatin.

Barrington, Arlington Heights, Rolling Meadows, Des Plaines—the names of the Chicago suburbs the Visitors had struck rolled through his head. The populations who had vanished overnight were here.

"Packed in individual serving containers," Janus gave voice to Walker's thoughts.

Walker's eyes narrowed when they shifted to Jennifer. "Are they dead?"

The woman's head lifted. "They are in what you humans call suspended animation."

"Waiting to be served as a snake feast!" Janus spat. "How many are here? Tens of thousands?"

"More. This is but one storage area on the ship." Her voice was a shamed whisper. "I can do nothing about them. But I can prevent you two from ending up here—or as Alicia's converts. We have to continue if we are going to catch the shuttle."

Before either Walker or Janus could protest, Jennifer turned and trotted down the wide catwalk. Walker's legs confirmed what his eyes had seen earlier when they finally reached the opposite end of the walkway. The catwalk did stretch for miles across the capsule-filled canyon.

Jennifer exited out a door similar to the one through which they had entered. Once in the main corridors, she took a left turn, walked to a four-way junction, turned left again, and stopped by a circular hatch. For the fifth time her fingers punched out a code on a panel of buttons.

Inside was another maintenance tunnel-shaft lined with the same pipes and wires Walker had seen in the first. However, the access point to the lower level was another thing entirely!

When she halted, it was beside a gaping rectangular shaft. The deafening roar of a hurricane came from within.

"It's the ventilation shaft," she shouted above the rush of air. "It's our only way down."

Walker edged to the shaft and peered down. A blast of frigid air, an Arctic-cold gale, slammed into his face. Blinking away tears that began to turn to icicles on his cheeks, he squinted and focused.

The shaft dropped away for a hundred feet. There he saw openings to the lower level on either side of the stainless steel well. Three thigh-thick pipes ran across the shaft from one opening to the other. Below that the shaft yawned downward forever. Walker's head turned from side to side, searching for a ladder. There was none.

"How in hell are we supposed to get down?" he yelled at the top of his lungs.

With a surprisingly strong arm, Jennifer pulled him away from the ventilation shaft. Slinging her rifle over a shoulder, she stood on the edge of the shaft, stretched legs and arms wide, then did a slow-motion fall into the shaft.

"No!" Walker's arm lashed out to grab the loose folds of her red uniform. His fingers snapped closed on empty air. In horror he watched the woman fall down the shaft.

The terror twisting his face abruptly washed away in a wide grin. Jennifer didn't fall; she floated. In her sky diver's position, the hurricane rush of air was almost a complete counterforce to her weight. Instead of plummeting to her death, she sank slowly down the shaft to gently alight on the pipes below. She turned, waved up at the two men above her, then crawled along the pipes into the opening on the opposite side of the shaft.

"Sam, I cannot . . ." Janus's face was white as a sheet, his eyes saucer wide.

"Yes, you can!" Walker shouted. "It's the only way. You'll do it even if I have to push you!"

Arm about his friend's waist, Walker tugged Janus to the gaping mouth of the shaft. "Now raise your arms and spread your legs!"

While the old man complied, Walker gave his back a nudge. Janus fell forward. Curses minutely detailing the younger man's parental relationship to a female dog, his preferred sexual partners, and the eternal destination of his soul yowled up the shaft while Janus floated down to land on the pipes. With Jennifer's helping hand, he crawled into the waiting opening.

Walker slung his rifle on his right shoulder, held arms and legs wide, and tumbled facedown into the icy blast of air. For an instant his stomach threatened to leap into his mouth. Then the air cushioned him. Like a feather on a gentle breeze, he drifted down to the pipes below. Seconds later he stood in the maintenance shaft, rubbing circulation back into his arms.

"Bay one lies outside that hatch." Jennifer pointed to an exit seventy-five feet down the service tunnel. "We have ten minutes to find and get ourselves aboard the shuttle. Lower your faceplates and remember to keep quiet!"

Walker slipped the rifle from his shoulder and double-checked its setting. If their flight through the Mother Ship had been some elaborate ruse, Alicia's trap awaited them outside the hatch. He snapped down his faceplate, waiting for his eyes to adjust to the nightlike darkness, and nodded for Jennifer to proceed.

Once through the hatch his apprehension tripled. Unlike their arrival on the Mother Ship, the landing bay now stood deserted except for three Visitors talking beside the open doors to a shuttle on their left. Walker's fingers curled around the trigger, ready to empty the weapon before he was taken again.

"We'll wait here until the two workers leave." Jennifer tilted her head toward the shuttle. "I'll handle the guard."

Mouth filled with cotton, Walker did the only thing he could—he waited. Minutes that seemed to stretch into hours dragged by. Eventually the two helmetless workers laughed, waved, and walked from the vehicle. Jennifer nodded and started forward with Walker and Janus at her heels.

"Private, you're assigned to guard duty here, not recreation period!" Jennifer's voice assumed the crisp military tone Walker had heard earlier. "Why are you fraternizing with workers?"

The shuttle's sole guard pivoted. His helmeted head

located Jennifer, and he snapped to rigid attention. In a blur of black, the woman's rifle jerked up. The butt of the weapon slipped beneath the edge of the faceplate to solidly connect with a concealed chin. The soldier crumpled to the ground with a grunt. Jennifer's muzzle swung about to cover him. He didn't move.

"If he twitches, fry him," she said, looking at Janus. Then to Walker she added, "Come with me. We've still got a pilot to deal with."

Walker darted into the open shuttle at her side. The lone pilot inside provided less of an obstacle than the guard. Jennifer merely pressed her rifle to his temple and threatened to empty his head of what little brains he possessed unless he did exactly as she ordered. With a gulp and a determined nod, he accepted her terms.

"Drag the guard inside," she ordered Walker. "We don't want him to be discovered, not when we're this close to escaping."

Without protest, Walker exited the craft and with Janus's help hauled the unconscious soldier into the squad vehicle. The craft's door closed behind them. Walker jerked around. Jennifer still stood with her rifle to the pilot's head. She hissed rapid-fire orders at the man in their native tongue.

The pilot obeyed without comment. His hands grasped a control lever at the side of his couch and moved it forward. The shuttle slipped across the landing bay, nosing toward the port that opened before the craft. He edged the lever down and the craft shot from the Mother Ship into the void of space.

"Get him and the guard into the storage compartment," Jennifer called out as she waved the pilot from the couch.

When Walker's muzzle motioned the man to the rear of the ship, Jennifer took the controls. She flicked a switch on the console in front of her. A hiss came from behind Walker.

He risked a glance. The storage compartment's door slid open.

Two minutes later the door eased back into place, locking pilot and unconscious guard inside. Walker lowered his rifle and sighed. For the first time since Jennifer had appeared in the doorway of their cell, he realized the woman was exactly what she claimed to be—a fifth columnist! There was no trap, only a friendly hand extended toward two total strangers.

Walker joined Jennifer in the nose of the shuttle. The motionless forms of the Visitor Mother Ships slipped by them outside. Ahead lay only darkness sprinkled with stars.

"You did it!" He grinned at the woman. "By damn, you did it!"

"We managed to get the shuttle, that's all." Jennifer tugged off her helmet. She shook her head; a cascade of brunette hair fell about her shoulders. There was no joy on her face when she glanced up at Walker. "We've still got to get you back home before Alicia discovers you're missing."

"You'll do it. If anyone can, you'll do it." He confidently squeezed her shoulder.

Jennifer's gaze returned to the panorama outside the craft. "With luck, Sam Walker."

Walker's jaw sagged when his own eyes shifted to the stars outside. A thin crescent of white formed in the darkness to his left—sunlight reflected from the surface of Earth's own moon! The Visitor invasion armada hadn't fled, merely taken one small step into space. They were hidden behind the moon.

As he stared in disbelief, a ball of blue marbled with white rose above the growing crescent. *Home*, he thought, basking in Earth's beauty. *We're going home!*

Chapter Nine

Walker's feet worked the control pedals while his hands shifted the levers on both sides of the pilot's couch. A blip of light on a minidisplay inset on the console slid two degrees off center of a circle that represented Earth. He reversed procedures and eased the shuttle back on course.

"A piece of cake!" He grinned at Jennifer. "This thing practically flies itself."

"In space all you have to do is lock your scanners on your destination and keep on course," she said, returning the smile. "However, in an atmosphere, the response is more like one of your own aircraft, only easier."

Like a child with a new toy on Christmas morning, Walker maneuvered the craft back and forth in a swinging arc. He wished for more control to fully test his ability with the shuttle, but with this particular squad vehicle, Alicia had eliminated the possibility of pilot hanky-panky.

Janus poked his head over Walker's shoulder, stared at the ever-increasing orb ahead of them, and asked, "Where do you intend to land this thing?"

"Navigational computer is locked on the outpost at

Arlington Park," Jennifer replied. "My attempts at overriding it have failed. We land where the computer takes us."

Walker bit at his lower lip. Jennifer had sketched the scene waiting for them on Earth. Gerald and his immune shock troopers were dug in at the abandoned racetrack. Arlington Park's isolation made it a perfect location for the first handhold in the Visitors' bid to regain control over humanity.

"I still do not understand how they expect to accomplish anything with only two hundred men." Janus shook his head. "The air, the water, the land itself is poisoned now. They can gain nothing."

"Alicia gains a center of operations, one she hopes will eventually allow her to retake Chicago and the Great Lakes." Jennifer slipped back into the pilot's couch when Walker stood. "Earth's wealth of water is too large a prize to simply abandon."

"But the V-Dust! Everything is poison to you!" Janus insisted.

"Your scientists developed an antitoxin." Jennifer turned to the old man. "Do you think ours can be that far behind?"

Janus's shocked expression equaled Walker's. The younger man's mind stumbled while he tried to accept what should have been obvious. The red toxin was humanity's only weapon against the Visitors' might. He had never considered the possibility of the aliens' developing an antitoxin of their own. Yet he now saw it as a very real probability. After all, this race of extraterrestrial reptiles had traveled over eight light-years to reach the Earth. The best of humankind's space efforts had only taken a few men to the surface of the moon.

"It's not water or food Alicia's after right now," Jennifer said. "She wants Paul Nordine and others."

"Nordine?" Walker's head snapped around, and he stared at the woman.

"She paves the way for her eventual return. One by one she plans to abduct Chicago's new leaders and convert them, starting with the head of the city's resistance," Jennifer explained. "You two were supposed to aid in kidnapping Nordine."

Ice flowed along Walker's spine. How simple Alicia's plan was! Who would suspect the Visitors could return to a poisoned world? How easy it would be to steal away those in power, convert them, then return them to the mainstream of life. No one would know, no one would guess—until the Visitors came to reclaim Earth again. Then it would be too late!

"That means there is a traitor in Chicago working with the lizard bitch!" Janus's blue eyes fired with anger.

"Possibly." Jennifer nodded. "More likely it's someone—or several ones—Alicia converted before our fleet was driven away. Remember the conversions started the day we arrived. Months went by before anyone even suspected that our commanders were molding the minds of your leaders."

"A traitor," Janus repeated. He scratched at the white stubble sprouted over his chin. "Who?" With a shake of his head, he stepped to the shuttle's interior and sank to the floor, lost in thought.

Walker ran a hand over his own cheeks, chin, and neck. The myriad of needlelike whiskers gave testimony to his own long absence from a razor. *A two days' growth,* he estimated in an attempt to pinpoint the time that had passed since Janus and he had been abducted. The beard wasn't the most accurate gauge, but it would have to do.

Lowering himself into a seat beside Jennifer, he stared at the sphere hanging in space ahead. The vague outlines of continents he had first learned on a globe in grammar school were now visible beneath the snowy cloud banks marbled across his world's surface.

Out here, the events of the last days seemed so distant, as though they belonged to another man who shared the name Samuel Walker. The Visitors' defeat, Kathleen's murder, the attack on the racetrack, Alicia's conversion chamber, Jennifer, the escape, all muddled in his brain while he attempted to piece together a plan of action for when they landed.

"After we touch down, couldn't we take off and fly into Chicago?" he asked while he gazed at the blue ball that was his home world.

"Computer's programmed to return to the Mother Ship on liftoff," Jennifer replied.

"Then we blow the damned computer," Walker said. "Blow it now and take manual control."

Jennifer shook her head. "These controls feed directly into the computer which interprets the pilot's commands for the drive. It's similar to the system on your own advanced jet fighters. The computer makes certain the pilot doesn't press the ship beyond its performance envelope."

"Damn Alicia and her flight programs!" Walker hammered a fist on the arm of his couch.

"She's afraid of defectors," Jennifer answered. "More and more of us are beginning to realize Our Great Leader lied about your people."

"And you?" Walker looked at the woman. "Are you among the recent converts to the fifth column movement?"

A soft chuckle reverberated in Jennifer's throat. "I *was* the fifth column aboard the Mother Ship when the fleet left our home world. I had opposed Our Great Leader long before he decided to invade Earth."

"Yet you came with the fleet, are one of Gerald's shock troopers." Walker stared at her, trying to probe beneath the human disguise she wore.

"My task was to organize opposition aboard our ship, to weaken the Leader's strength from within." Her green eyes darted to Walker. "In all honesty, I did it for my own people, not yours. Human beings were of no concern to me until I met the people of Earth. Then I realized Our Great Leader had once again lied to us."

She explained that she had discovered a traitor among the fifth columnists and planned to assassinate him during the battle confusion on V-Day. "You know him. He's called Gerald. However, the battle we expected never came. I never got close enough to him."

"You did get an antitoxin tablet," Walker said, realizing Jennifer had been among the force who had struck resistance headquarters in Lake Zurich.

Jennifer nodded. "I thought Alicia would eliminate Gerald for distributing the antitoxin. Instead, he's now the spearhead for her new invasion of your planet. I am letting him live until I'm certain of Alicia's plans."

"Now you're saving the necks of two strangers instead of dealing with him," Walker said. "What if something happens to us? Surely you're needed on the Mother Ship."

Jennifer shrugged and smiled. "Saving two lives seems more important than taking one. As to the Mother Ship, there are others among our numbers as capable as I—more so. I will be missed, but our efforts will not end. And once we've landed, I'm in your hands, yours and Janus's."

"Our hands?" Walker stared at her, uncertain what she meant.

He grimaced when her meaning penetrated. For two utter strangers, Jennifer had sacrificed her world. In freeing them from the cell and piloting them to Earth, Jennifer had completely cut herself off from the Mother Ship and her own people. There was no turning back for her now. Not with the two witnesses against her packed away in the storage compartment.

"Isn't there a way we could dump the two in the back before we land?" Walker asked. "That might give you a chance. You could say we jumped you, forced you to pilot us home."

Walker detected a sadness in her eyes and in the way the corners of her mouth hung when she looked at him again. "Would that explain the guards back at your cell? They can identify me."

She paused and drew a heavy breath. "No, my friend. The two in the back will live. Even if killing them would help me, I'm afraid I couldn't do it. They are merely carrying out orders. They know no better."

"Yet you would kill Gerald?"

"*He* is different." Her lips drew thin and tight. "He knows what he does. For him my people and your people mean nothing. The bodies of the dead are merely stepping stones for him."

Walker sank back in his seat and stared out the wide viewport that spanned the front of the shuttle. While he had hidden away in his stall, some insidious spider had spun an intricate web that had ensnared the people of two worlds. How petty humankind's own bickering and wars seemed when compared to this conflict that stretched across the stars.

"I wish there was something I could say, something I could offer in return for what you are doing for us," he finally said.

"I won't be alone." Jennifer smiled and tried to sound lighthearted. "There are others like myself on your planet. Other fifth columnists who chose to stay and help those they came to conquer. I won't be alone."

How many Visitors remained on Earth? Walker had no idea. He had only heard them mentioned once or twice since the Visitors' fleet had fled Earth's atmosphere. Were they so different from the human beings he had seen trapped in the gelatin-filled cocoons on the Mother Ship?

"The people we saw packed away in the storage area," Walker said, "what happens to them?"

"Nothing, at least for the moment. They will remain in suspended animation until the fleet returns to our home."

"But I thought we were the same as cattle to your race? That we were being harvested?"

Jennifer nodded. "That was to be the fate of your whole planet, but not until the Mother Ships returned to the star you call Sirius. For those of us in the ships, we brought up laboratory animals—rabbits, mice, rats, birds. If we had proceeded down the last corridor we walked instead of entering bay one, you would have seen the cages and pens in which the animals are bred."

A sigh of relief escaped Walker's lips. For the time being the men, women, and children aboard the Mother Ships were safe.

"Do you find our eating habits that repulsive?" Jennifer arched an eyebrow.

"Aside from the fact I've never been on a dinner menu before, yes. Rats and mice aren't exactly what I call appetizing." Walker shivered at the thought of eating either.

Jennifer pursed her lips thoughtfully. "But your race eats meat. Is there any difference?"

"A beef steak is a far cry from a raw rat," Walker protested.

"I've tasted your beef. How do you like it prepared, Samuel Walker?" Jennifer's gaze shifted from the control panel to him.

"Rare and bloody," Walker said, then shrugged in chagrin when a smile crept across Jennifer's lips.

"How long until we touch down?" Walker changed subjects.

"We're midway between your moon and Earth." Jennifer nodded at a display with alien characters on the console. "Another two hours before we reach Arlington Park."

Walker did some quick addition. "Four hours from the moon to the earth?"

Jennifer nodded. "Perhaps you should take advantage of the time remaining the way your friend Janus is doing."

She tilted her head over her right shoulder. Walker followed the direction of the gesture and saw Janus stretched out on the floor of the shuttle, snoring loudly.

"I might just do that." Walker snuggled down in the couch and closed his eyes. He knew he wouldn't sleep, but he needed time to be alone with his thoughts, needed time to sort through everything Jennifer had said, and place it in perspective.

Chapter Ten

The Visitor shuttle fell. Beneath the white segmented length of its body, the face of humankind's home world rushed by in a dizzy blur. The blues of the oceans, the mountain ranges of snowy clouds, the greens and browns of continents streaked by one another.

Walker's pulse throbbed at an ever-increasing rate. The pounding rhythm in his temples boomed in counterbeat to the sharp, gasping intakes of his breath. For the thousandth time since their abduction, the former Vietnam helicopter pilot stood face to face with the reality of his situation. The Visitor squad vehicle was no chopper, nor was the airless void of space either the humid air of Southeast Asia or Los Angeles's smog-clogged sky.

We're falling too damned fast! Beads of sweat popped out on his brow when he turned to Jennifer. She sat beside him in the pilot's chair with her gaze focused outside beyond the blunt nose of the craft. Her hands barely rested on the shuttle's controls. The two levers moved without so much as an involuntary twitch of her hands or arms. The shuttle's computer was in total control now.

Walker shook his head, trying to push away the rising panic that knotted within his chest. Even closing his eyes didn't help. Countless images of the NASA reentry simulations he had watched on television since childhood crowded his mind. In these the spacecraft plummeted toward earth, heat shield glowing red then white hot from the atmospheric friction. *Hell, I don't even known if this bucket has a heat shield!*

"Take a deep breath and relax." Jennifer attempted to comfort him.

Walker followed her suggestion. His pulse still pounded like a madman beating a bass drum.

"I told you this thing practically flies itself." Jennifer flashed him a reassuring smile. "Even if I wanted to plunge head-on into the atmosphere, I couldn't. The computer won't interpret a command that could endanger the ship."

Walker swallowed. "Yeah, I know that's what you said. Trouble is, my stomach doesn't believe it."

"Should have slept like I suggested." Her sympathetic smile widened. She nodded to the interior of the shuttle where Janus sprawled on the floor, sleeping like a baby. "Tell your stomach to hold on a few more minutes. The worst part is almost over."

Walker did that. His stomach gave a quivery rumble in reply.

Outside daylight transformed to dusk, then to the darkness of night. The craft shot about the earth's curvature. The fiery glow of reentry Walker expected never came. The shuttle just continued to plummet toward the dark face of humanity's home world. Here and there below, he saw patches of light marking the cities and towns that had survived the Visitors' reign of terror.

"That's Chicago." Jennifer tilted her head toward an elongated swatch of illumination directly ahead of the shuttle's nose. "Better wake Janus. We'll be touching down within ten minutes."

Knees threatening to turn liquid on him, Walker cautiously stood, steadied himself, then moved to the old man's side. A gentle nudge to his friend's shoulder and Janus's eyes opened wide.

"Anything wrong?" Janus pushed to his elbows. His gaze darted about like that of a man trying to remember where he was.

"Not yet." Walker shook his head. "But we're about to jump into the frying pan. Ten minutes until we land."

Helping Janus to his feet, Walker returned to the nose of the shuttle. The scene outside quelled the uneasy churnings of his stomach. No longer did the world rush by in a color-streaking blur. Instead the craft glided steadily toward Chicago's lights. The squad vehicle now possessed the familiar feel of an aircraft on a landing approach rather than a meteor plummeting toward earth.

"Have they learned of our escape?" Janus leaned on the back of Walker's couch and stared into the night outside.

"I've monitored all communiqués from the Mother Ship," Jennifer replied. "Unless Alicia's come up with a code that's unknown to me, there's been no mention of our escape."

"That will give us a little time when we land," Walker said.

"Not much. They'll be onto us the moment they open the storage compartment and see our two passengers back there," Jennifer replied.

"Still, we'll have a chance at making it to Janus's car," Walker answered, purposely omitting the rest of the thought that entered his mind. *If the Pinto is still there*.

A barely perceivable tremble ran through the shuttle as it lowered speed and nosed downward. Walker tried to make out familiar landmarks in the darkness below. From the air the ground below appeared estranged and alien. Only when the long rows of Arlington Park's barns came into sight was Walker certain of their position.

"I see no one below." Janus sucked at his teeth when the shuttle leveled and skimmed over the racetrack's stable area. "Maybe they have left."

Neither Jennifer nor Walker mentioned the obvious—a supply shuttle wasn't sent to an abandoned outpost. However, Walker did point to the empty parking lot that had held Janus's car.

"Our best bet is to make a try for one of the barns," he said. "That will give us some cover. Then we'll have to play it by ear."

"I still see no one," Janus said from behind him. "Where are Gerald's troops?"

"They're waiting until we land before coming out," Jennifer answered.

Walker's mind raced. If Jennifer was right, that just might give them the edge they needed. "Will this thing land itself?"

Jennifer nodded, an eyebrow arching in question.

"Then we're not going to wait for Gerald's playmates to come out and greet us. The instant the shuttle sets down, we're going to make a run for those barns." Walker pointed at a single line of stables on the north edge of the parking lot. "If we can make it that far, we've got a chance of getting out of the track under the fence."

Motioning Janus back into the shuttle, Walker pushed from his couch with Jennifer following right behind him. Together, rifles unslung and primed, they waited for the slight vibration that ran through the ship when it touched down on the parking lot. The craft's door swung open.

Walker leaped to the ground before the lower portion of the door met the pavement. His rifle swung from side to side, covering possible attack. Nothing but the night greeted him.

"Run," his urgent whisper hissed. He waved Janus north. Then to Jennifer, "Move it!"

"With you," the woman answered.

Walker's gaze shot to her. The curses on his tongue went unspoken. Opening stall doors creaked from beyond the low white fence that edged the parking lot. Walker gave a jerk of his head and ran after Janus. In powerful, fluid strides Jennifer matched his pace.

Halfway to the protection of the northern stables, a voice from behind shouted, "Halt!" Walker bowed his head and kept running. The next sound he heard was the single command, "Fire!"

The crackle of bolts spitting from the barrels of energy fires swallowed the night's silence. Walker darted right then left in zigzagging strides. Blue-white globes of pulse-beam death danced through the air about him. Flowers of fire blossomed on the pavement as the bolts missed their marks and slammed into the ground.

Fifty yards, twenty-five—Walker mentally counted off the distance separating him from the barn Janus ducked into ahead. A few more seconds of luck and he and Jennifer would be . . .

Jennifer? His head jerked to the right. The woman no longer ran at his side. *Where the* . . .

An anguished curse from behind him answered the question before it fully formed in his mind. He spun around. Jennifer knelt twenty-five feet behind him, clutching her right shoulder.

Walker reacted rather than thought. His rifle's barrel leaped up; his finger squeezed the trigger. A stream of sizzling energy bolts blasted into the barrage of Visitor fire that attempted to home in on him.

"Out!" Jennifer waved him toward the barn. "Get out of here, damn you!"

"I've got you covered," Walker shouted. "Get to the barn!"

With another jerk of her arm, she turned back to the small

army of advancing shock troopers swarming from the barns. She reached down with her left hand, lifted her rifle from the ground, and opened fire on the soldiers.

Walker heard four screams echo from the Visitor force before three energy bolts converged on Jennifer's kneeling form. Then there was no reason for his covering fire—only the lifeless body of an alien woman sprawled on the pavement, a woman who had given her life to save two total strangers.

Wheeling about, Walker sprinted across the open concrete to the safety of the barn. He answered Janus's questioning stare with a single word—"Dead"—then pushed the older man to the other side of the shedrow.

Out of the shock troopers' line of fire, they now ran from the barn and into the shadows of the next, then on to the next. Walker cursed with each stride he took. The drainage ditch exit under the fence that surrounded the track lay behind them. To make a try for it would be suicidal. Janus and he had to put some distance between the soldiers and themselves. They needed time to scale the barrier of chain-linked steel or to blast their way through it.

Walker halted at the receiving barn, where winning thoroughbreds had once been brought for standard veterinary checks of saliva and urine and for the use of illegal drugs. Shouts and the crunch of booted feet came out of the night ahead of them.

"Damn! Gerald's troops must be spread out all over the track!" His eyes darted to the north and the fence standing but a few yards away.

So close but so far! He realized they would never make it over or through the fence before the shock troopers in front and behind reached them. To make a stand here would be equally insane.

"The grandstand!" Walker urged Janus to the south and the dark silhouette towering there. "If we can make it across the center field, we'll try the fence on the opposite side of the track!"

He failed to mention that before they reached the grandstand, they had to cross another open parking lot. Gerald's forces did not overlook that fact. A barrage of energy bolts sliced through the darkness around them when they eventually reached the cover of the paddock.

Together the two men ducked behind the walls of the paddock. They gulped down two lungfuls of air, rose, and sprayed a stream of bolts into the soldiers behind them. Wasting no further time, they darted for the entry tunnel that ran through the grandstand and onto the sandy racecourse on the opposite side.

Janus's arm snaked out and grabbed Walker's shoulder when they reached the track. He pointed to the center field.

"Snakes!"

A line of shock troopers hastened across the open field at the center of the track.

"They've got us cut off on all sides!" Panic tightened the older man's voice.

Walker saw no soldiers to the east. However, he wasn't willing to risk their lives on the chance Gerald hadn't stationed men there. The Visitor officer had put them everywhere else!

"Into the grandstand. We've got to find a place to hide." Walker vaulted over the waist-high wire fence that separated the track from the grandstand.

While Janus scrambled over the wire barrier, Walker scanned the darkened structure. The rows of seats and benches, the box seats, the betting windows inside were too obvious. The Visitors would search them all. He needed a place that would be overlooked.

His neck craned back to the lofty slanting roof overhanging the grandstand. A humorless smile played on his lips. Tucked just beneath the outer edge of the roof was a small windowed box—the race announcer's booth. His eyes moved behind the booth to a catwalk running beneath the roof. Along the back of the grandstand a metal stairway zigzagged up the wall to the catwalk.

Pointing to the stairway, Walker ran into the grandstand with Janus at his side. The announcer's booth was risky, but it was a chance, and it was all they had.

By the time the two men reached the stairs, the echo of scrambling footsteps rang through the deserted structure. Sending Janus up to the first level, Walker waited below with rifle level and ready to cover him. In turn, the older man covered his companion's climb. They worked up, reaching the catwalk unnoticed. Crouched low, they crept across the catwalk, opened the door to the booth, and slipped inside.

"We are trapped here if they decide to come up for a look." Janus sank to the floor with his back to a wall, gulping for air.

Walker didn't reply. His gaze took in their hiding place. The booth was small and cramped. A long, desklike shelf ran across the front length of the small room. Six metal folding chairs were shoved beneath the shelf. The walls only rose to his waist. The rest was window glass rising to the ceiling.

Pressing his head against one of the windows, Walker glanced above.

Overhead stretched a network of steel girders that supported the massive roof. For an instant Walker considered the possibility of climbing into the girders and working to the roof's edge. There they could pull themselves on top of the roof.

He glanced down. Like black ants, shock troopers scurried back and forth, searching the rows of seats below.

He bit at his lower lip. A try for the girders would be a one-way ticket into oblivion. The only way to get at the

network of steel was through a window. And the only way
out a window was to break one, an action that would train
every rifle below on the announcer's booth.

Besides, he thought, pushing the idea away, *I've no
guarantee Janus could make the climb*. Although his friend
didn't complain about the missing finger, even now the older
man sat with his injured hand protectively cradled in his lap.

"What are they doing?"

Janus's voice drew Walker's attention from the window.
He sank down to the floor and sighed. "Wondering how two
men could vanish into thin air," he replied.

"They will look for us here, Sam," Janus said. "It might
take Gerald time to even realize this booth exists, but he is
thorough. His men will come for us."

"Time is all I want right now. Give us a chance to catch
our breaths and maybe come up with a way to get out of
here with our hides in one piece." Walker's gaze coursed
about the cramped room once again. Eventually his eyes
rose to the girders. "Just need a little time to think, Janus.
Just a little time to think."

"We have trouble," Janus said as he dropped to the floor.
He had been peering out a window. "Snakes are climbing
the stairs."

Walker crawled across the floor and peeked out the
window. A line of shock troopers wove up the zigzagging
metal stairs. They had already reached the third level. In the
two hours Janus and he had hidden in the booth, no miracle
plan of escape had burst full-blown into his mind. Now their
short reprieve had run out.

"At least we have the high ground." Walker scooted
across to the door and edged it open. He cursed. "Can't get
a shot at them from here. Catwalk's in the way."

Janus nodded to the windows on each side of the door.

"They will offer us little protection when the fighting begins. I see no reason to keep them. The snakes know we are here."

Walker studied his friend, saw the fear that drew his features taut. "We could wait until they reach the catwalk."

"As you said, Sam, we have the high ground," Janus replied. "We should not waste such an advantage."

Janus slowly stood and lifted his rifle. Walker nodded and pushed from the floor, hefting his rifle. Together they slammed the butts of their weapons into the windowpanes. Glass showered out, tinkling down into the yawning darkness.

A moment later they turned the rifles on the ascending column of soldiers. They used the alien firearms like machine guns. Pulse bursts of energy globes sizzled across the grandstand. Flames flowered along the metal stairway and the wall behind it. Screams and shouts rolled upward.

As to the actual damage their volley did, Walker couldn't be certain. Each blue bolt that spat from his barrel was like an exploding camera flash, blinding him to the world beyond the fuzzy aurora of light filling his eyes.

Glass shattered behind him. Walker ducked, hugged the wall, and threw his arms over his head. A barrage of answering bolts hissed up at them. Again and again the blasts struck home, eliminating the windows that had barred their escape into the girders only a second before.

For an eternity Walker crouched there waiting for the glass to quit breaking. Another eternity passed before the crackle of energy bolts stopped. Walker's arms slowly came away from his head, and he glanced at Janus.

Terror now gripped the old man's face. His whole body trembling, Janus scooted from the corner and slid across the floor to the open door. He turned back to Walker and said, "They are still coming. I can hear them on the steps."

"Then I suggest we give them another round." Walker started to rise.

"No, it is no good, my friend. We cannot stop them." Janus's eyes rolled to the girders. "I have seen you looking at the steel beams. Do you think you can climb to them?"

"I don't know." There was something in Janus's voice Walker had never heard before. "Why?"

"Because there is a chance for one of us to get out of here and warn Paul of Alicia's plot," Janus replied in a still tone that belied his quaking body. "I cannot make the climb, not with this."

He held his left hand inches from Walker's face.

"No," Walker answered, his voice just as determined as Janus's. "I won't leave you here."

"You will." Janus raised the muzzle of his rifle, centering it on Walker's chest. "You must, before they reach the catwalk."

Walker's head moved from side to side. "Go ahead and shoot. I'm not leaving you."

For a moment, Walker thought the old man might squeeze the trigger. Then Janus's shoulders slumped and the rifle lowered.

"Do not do this thing to me, Sam." There were tears in Janus's words. "Do not rob me of this final chance to prove myself a man."

"What in hell are you talking about?" Walker's forehead furrowed. "This isn't the time to—"

"It is all the time I have." Janus's head jerked up, and his gaze locked onto his friend. "I am a man of big words, Sam. All of them lies. In the old country, the lies began. When I was young, I was a coward. While family and friends fought Hitler's storm troopers, I hid. They died and I lived."

He paused and swallowed. "I wanted to fight. But I could not. I was too frightened of death, of pain. So I lived. But it has been a life of nightmares haunted by those loved ones. Each night I relive their deaths, their anguish. How many times I have prayed for death."

Walker stared at his friend. He couldn't believe what he was hearing.

"Paul Nordine offered me the opportunity to redeem myself," Janus continued. "The old fears returned. Instead of fighting, I hid just as surely as you did. No battles for Janus Brodaski, no chance of death. I became an observer and hid among the ruins left by the Visitors."

"But—" Walker tried to cut in.

"No 'buts,' my friend. I know what I was. Now I have the chance to change that." Janus pleaded now. "Please do not rob me of that chance! Go! Try for the girders!"

"Janus . . ." Walker's intended words trailed away unspoken as his friend's gaze held him. Like it or not, there was a chance for one of them to make the girders and then the roof. But just one of them, and only if the other provided cover fire.

"Sam, please. Do not steal this time from me. Let my life count for something. Please. Go now. Get away before it is too late. It is in your hands now. Get to Paul and warn him."

In my hands. Walker felt his gut knot. That was the second time this night he had been told that. Jennifer said it first, and she was dead, cut down by the weapons of her own people. Now Janus signed his own death warrant with the same phrase. Yet, there was no way Walker could escape the truth of their situation. One of them might make it to the roof.

Walker nodded and held his rifle out to his friend. "At least take this. You might need it."

"No, I think my own rifle might be more than I will have use of, my friend." A sad little smile moved across the old man's lips. "Take the rifle with you, and go now. We have wasted too much time."

Slinging the rifle over a shoulder, Walker reached out, took Janus's trembling hand, and squeezed it. Tearing his

gaze from the old man's face, Walker scooted to the back of
the room and crouched by the long shelf. He looked back at
Janus and nodded again.

No sound passed Janus's lips, no final words. He simply
shoved to his feet, swung the rifle to one of the broken
windows, aimed below, and fired at the column of Visitors
who wound up the metal stairway.

Walker saw no more. With the first blast from his friend's
weapon, he leaped atop the wooden shelf and moved to its
outer edge. He glanced once at the two-hundred-foot drop
to the ground, then reached up. The fingers of his right hand
lipped over the top of the booth and secured a hold. Sucking
in a steady breath, he lifted his left hand, caught the top of
the structure, and pulled himself up.

Torso and legs swung like a precarious pendulum in the
night while he inched one elbow then the other over the top
of the announcer's booth. He cursed. The space between the
booth's roof and the girders was too narrow for him to crawl
between. The only way was up!

Stretching his right arm out, he wrapped it around a steel
beam. He shoved away from the booth's roof with his left
hand and snaked the arm out, catching the girder. For a
moment he hung there, legs swinging back and forth in
empty air. Above the pounding in his temples he heard the
sizzling bolts of Janus's cover fire and the screaming and
shouting that rose from below.

Walker's muscles tautened. Inch by inch he hauled
himself atop the girder until he collapsed belly down on its
flat surface. He allowed himself five deep breaths before
glancing overhead. The girder on which he balanced was
part of a crisscross understructure for the main support
beams of the grandstand's roof. Only two feet separated him
from the underside of the roof. Again his only course was
out and up. He began to worm his way across the steel
toward the edge of the roof.

Light like a thousand tracer bullets ripping through the night soared from below. He risked a glance. Gerald's army of shock troopers returned Janus's volley. Here and there a wild shot flamed against the grandstand's roof, but nothing more. His progress went unnoticed; the lizards didn't see him.

At the end of the girder, Walker cautiously rolled to his back, hooked his right arm over the edge of the roof, and then his left. He pulled out and up, easing his chest, then his legs onto the roof. A smile moved over lips while his body threatened to go liquid—he had done it! He had made it to the roof!

Now all he had to do was find a way down.

Pushing to his feet, he scrambled to the back edge of the slightly slanting roof. There he found the descending avenue he sought. A maintenance ladder led down.

His gaze surveyed the ground below. His eyes told him the same thing as the shouts and the crackling hiss of energy bolts coming from within the grandstand: the guards had abandoned their posts. Gerald's entire force was inside the structure trying to take the announcer's booth.

Swinging his feet onto the ladder's rungs, Walker started down. A scream—a human scream—cut through the night.

Janus! Walker clung to the rungs, tears welling in his eyes. No sound except for reverberating Visitor voices and the clang of booted feet on metal stairs came from within the grandstand. *Gone!*

. . . in your hands . . .

Janus's and Jennifer's voices drifted through Walker's mind, urging him on. The time for sorrow would be later—if there was a later. Two rungs at a time, he climbed down the ladder. The moment his feet hit the ground, he turned and ran east. Ten minutes later he scrambled to freedom over the chain-link fence that encircled the racetrack.

Chapter Eleven

Walker stared behind him. Two miles to the west, he saw Visitor squad vehicle lights scanning the racetrack below. *Two miles,* he thought as he sucked at his cheeks. The distance gave him breathing room—but not much.

Three, perhaps four, of the shuttlecraft floated in the air. It wouldn't take that long for Gerald and his men to realize he had fled the track. And there was only one way for Walker to go if he intended to warn Paul Nordine. Even searching as they went, it would be an hour, maybe two, before the ships overtook a man on foot.

Walker did not intend to remain on foot. Turning, he perused the residential street before him, the second such street he had entered. Automobiles lined the curbs and sat in driveways like obedient pets awaiting the return of their masters.

A shiver worked up Walker's spine while he walked to the nearest car. Those masters now lay encased in gelatin-filled, plastic cocoons aboard Alicia's Mother Ship. In suspended animation they awaited transportation to an alien world orbiting distant Sirius where they were to be bred and slaughtered like cattle.

Reaching the car, he lifted its hood and across the battery posts placed a piece of wire he had yanked from one of the fifty cars he had already tried. Nothing. He moved to the next vehicle and repeated the process. Again nothing.

He crossed the street to a blue pickup, only to achieve the same results. In spite of the barrage of television commercials that once loudly proclaimed the longevity of car batteries, six months of inactivity had taken its toll. Drained of the life that had sparked them, the dust-covered vehicles were little more than useless shells of glass and steel, reminders of a world that existed before the Visitors' arrival.

Undaunted by his repeated failures, Walker worked down the street from car to car, from curb to driveway, from driveway to curb. As he bent over an '84 Caprice, a spark crackled beneath the hood.

Walker caught his breath as he leaped back. Incredulously he stared at the massive engine. He stepped forward, lifted the wire from the battery, and touched it to the posts again. Blue and hot, a spark popped.

Tossing aside the wire, he slammed down the hood and trotted to the driver's side of the sedan. He pressed in the door's button and tugged. The door refused to budge.

With a muttered curse, he brushed the dust from the window and leaned close. Another curse escaped his lips. The lock stem inside was one of those sleek, shiny rods intended to prevent theft. There was no way he could pull the stem up with something like a looped coat hanger—even if he had a coat hanger!

Walker used the only tool available to him. He aimed the rifle at the window and pulled the trigger. Exploding blue-white energy leaped from the muzzle and glass shattered. Not waiting for the strobe-light effect of the shot to fade from his eyes, he probed an arm into the now-open window, found the push-button lock, pressed it, then jerked on the door handle. The car's interior lights came on bright and beaming, testimony to the battery's strength.

Now let the gas tank be full! He dusted aside the shattered glass on the seat then slid inside. The distinctive new-car smell wafted in his nostrils as he ducked his head beneath the dashboard. A few moments of educated probing and lucky guesses produced the ignition wires. Tugging the wires from the dash as far as he could, he leaned down and used teeth and fingernails to strip away their plastic coatings.

The copper wires bare, he sat up. Drawing a deep breath and releasing it in a whispered prayer, he gently depressed the gas pedal twice, three times—then touched the exposed wires together.

The engine coughed once, then did nothing. He tapped the gas and pressed the wires again. The engine ground, groaning in loud protest as it tried to turn over. Another nudge of the accelerator and it caught, vibrating unevenly until he eased the gas forward once more. Then it purred like some great cat.

Carefully twisting the ignition wires together, Walker glanced at the dashboard. The fuel gauge swung all the way right to the white "F." Confidence reborn in his breast, he tried the windshield washer and wipers. Both worked, quickly removing the months of grime from the glass.

His hand moved to the headlight knob. When his fingers touched the cool chrome, he jerked them away. A nervous whistle escaped his lips. Old habits had almost given his position away. One glimpse of headlight beams and the Visitor squad vehicles would swarm over him like hornets.

He switched on the radio. Some nameless voice on a local station told him it was four A.M., partly cloudy, 68 degrees, with a 40 percent chance of summer showers before the day was over. Promising news headlines on the half hour, the same voice proclaimed less talk and more music and began an hour of moldy oldies beginning with Chuck Berry's classic "Maybellene."

With the early rock and roller singing about chasing his unfaithful lover down the highway, Walker slammed the door, eased the Caprice into drive, and pulled from the curb. Fifteen minutes, and four songs by the Beach Boys, Paul McCartney, the Rolling Stones, and Wilson Pickett, later he wheeled onto the Northwest Tollway and headed east toward Chicago.

After a brief interruption for a public service announcement detailing the food-rationing procedures for Chicago's residents, the disk jockey went into music again, starting with Jan and Dean's "Deadman's Curve."

Walker smiled. He vaguely recalled the song that had reached an oldie but goldie status by the time he entered high school. Further, he remembered his father teasing him about staying away from "deadman's curve" the day he had purchased his first car.

Panic gripped Walker when the '60s duo began the second verse of their drag-racing saga. His panic had nothing to do with the song's lyrics. His lower molars throbbed in unison with the back beat.

Eyes shifting to rear-view and side mirrors, he scanned the sky behind him. There was no sign of a squad vehicle. The pulse of his teeth spread toward the front of this mouth, but still the mirrors remained empty.

Walker's right foot nudged the accelerator toward the floorboard. In the next instant, he jerked the foot from the gas and stomped on the brake pedal.

Rubber screamed against concrete. The front of the Caprice dipped as the brakes grabbed, then locked. The car skidded. Smoke rose from its front tires an instant before it swung halfway around and shuddered to a halt.

Bolts of eye-blinding blue erupted overhead. A twin line of pulse-beam bursts bit harmlessly into the highway ahead of the vehicle. Moonlight glinted off a shuttle's angular body as it shot overhead and disappeared into the night.

Damning the proficiency of Gerald's search, Walker wrenched the steering wheel around. Heading the car east, he jammed the gas pedal to the floor. Gaze riveted to the distant point where the craft had vanished, he managed to steer around the looming hulk of an overturned bus without slowing his speed. The dot of dim light he knew would return flickered back in the sky.

His hands tightened around the steering wheel. His pulse tripled its racing pace while the white form grew with each passing second.

He repressed the panicky urge to swing the car off the road in a desperate search for a building to shelter him. The action would be certain suicide. The cover of the building would be like walking into a cage. Once he was on foot again, the shock troopers in the squad vehicle would have him. His best chance was here on the road, mobile and maneuverable.

Energy bolts leaped from the nose of the approaching shuttle. Walker gritted his teeth. The craft swooped low, strafing the road as it came. That this was the exact tactic he expected didn't improve his position, only gave him a slight edge—a very slight edge.

Eyes ahead, foot to the floor, he drove directly toward the dual beams of pulsing force. Even above the roar of the wind rushing through the car's broken window he heard the hot anger of the bolts striking the pavement.

And he waited.

Fifty feet ahead of his path the deadly globes of energy slammed into the highway. He spun the steering wheel to the left. Tires screamed in protest as the Caprice veered toward the shoulder of the road to avoid the strafing bolts.

To *almost* avoid the strafing bolts!

A fist hammered down from above and struck the rear of the car with bone-jarring force. The car bucked and lurched violently. Blue-white light bathed the interior of the Chevy. Riding out the invisible hands that attempted to wrench the steering wheel from his grip, Walker regained control and steered back to the center of the highway.

He glanced in the rear-view mirror and paled. Within the car's trunk was wedged the scorched and crumpled remnants of its hood. A sickening, cold nausea swept through Walker's stomach. He had been lucky. The trunk's hood had absorbed the force of the impact, preventing the bolt's energy from reaching the gas tank and turning the car—and him—into a Roman candle.

The luck riding his shoulders wouldn't remain there, he realized. Were he sitting at the controls of the squad vehicle, Walker would abandon the jet-jockey tactics after two failed strafing runs. The shuttlecraft could also perform helicopter-imitating maneuvers. It would be much easier to ride the car's tail and lob shots below. Marksmanship wasn't needed for the task, just patience. Sooner or later one of the blasts would strike home.

"Bastards!" Walker slammed a fist into the seat beside him.

The squad vehicle's familiar blunt snout appeared in the rear-view mirror, dropping from above. Once again his ability to second-guess the pilot's maneuver gave him little comfort. He cut the steering wheel to the right. The Caprice responded, veering sharply.

Two bolts burst from the nose of the shuttle and flamed to the empty road where Walker had been only a moment ago.

The instant the craft began to slide through the air to regain its position behind the Chevy, Walker wheeled the car to the left. The pilot's next shots burned into the highway's right shoulder.

Five more zigs and zags and sweat rolled from Walker's brow. Each burst from the shuttle's dual guns inched closer to the car. The pilot was starting to anticipate his movements. The high-speed death waltz would end in another few quick turns.

Unless I take the lead. Walker lifted the rifle from the seat beside him. Shifting if from his right to left arm, he angled the barrel outside the glassless window and pointed the muzzle toward the starry sky. His right foot jumped from gas pedal to brake.

The squad vehicle shot over him. His finger squeezed down on the trigger. A line of blue bursts leaped into the air, missing their mark. Pressing the accelerator to the floor once more, Walker swung the rifle about, following the craft as it banked and soared up. The globelike bolts sailed uselessly into the air.

Walker had time for one easy breath before the shuttle dropped behind him again, hanging farther back this time, eliminating his chance at another braking maneuver. The jerking, zigzagging dance from one side of the highway to the other began anew.

And was abruptly interrupted when the Caprice shot beneath an overpass. The shuttle's pilot nearly ended Walker's worries by almost plowing his ship into the bridge of concrete and steel. But the craft did what Walker swore was a 90-degree turn and shot up into the night.

Walker's mind raced, turning over the seed of an idea planted there. He had been wrong about needing cover earlier. At least, wrong about the type of protection he needed. A house or a building wouldn't serve for what he planned. However, what he did need lay directly ahead near O'Hare.

For a third time, the shuttle dropped behind the Chevy. With determination, Walker resumed the deadly game of duck and dodge with the energy bolts that blasted from the craft's nose. A grim, humorless smile twisted his lips when he saw his destination rise before him. Cloverleaf interchanges loomed above the tollway where several highways converged on the airport.

Veering out of the line of another twin bolt from the shuttle, he shot beneath the Mixmaster of curving and arching roadways. The shuttle arced upward, glided over the interchanges, and dropped to the opposite side of the crisscrossing interchange.

Only Walker wasn't there. Braking, he came to a halt in the center of the highway and sat there with his motor idling and fingers crossed.

To the east the squad vehicle veered in a wide circle and came rushing back to the cloverleafs. The glaring bolts of blue strafed from the sky and exploded harmlessly against the network of roads woven above the Chevy. The shuttle shot up and over the interchanges, circled, and tried again from the west—with the same results. Twice more the Visitor craft's strafing runs failed.

When the squad vehicle returned from the east for the third time, it hovered in the air as though those inside were pondering how to flush out their prey.

There's only one way to get me, Walker thought while he studied the motionless ship. *Come in and get me, you bastards. Come in and get me!*

As though obeying his silent command, the vessel sank toward the pavement. Walker's breath hissed between his teeth. The moment of truth had arrived. The pilot had two choices—land or fly beneath the tangle of overpasses. Either way Walker was prepared to deal with the situation.

The grim smile returned to his lips. Had he been at the controls of the shuttle, he would have risked a flight beneath the interchange. The squad vehicle's pilot didn't. His craft lightly touched the ground and squatted there like an overgrown dragonfly minus its wings.

Walker waited.

The doors on the shuttle's side swung up and down simultaneously.

The time for waiting had passed. Walker gunned the Caprice, his foot slamming the accelerator to the floorboard. Rubber peeled in two black strips on the concrete behind him. The speedometer needle leaped toward the right side of its range.

Mouth suddenly cotton dry, Walker mentally counted off the distance between him and the squad vehicle. He reached down, pulled the headlight knob, and flicked the beam to bright. Rifle secure in his right hand, he opened the door with his left. Without a glance at the blurred highway that rushed by outside, he rolled from the car.

Pain lanced through his left shoulder when he tumbled onto the pavement. He cried out, his scream drowned in a deafening explosion as the Caprice slammed into the shuttle.

Heat and flame blossomed, boiling in a monstrous ball that consumed the two vehicles. One glance at the fiery inferno he had created was all Walker got. In the next instant, he threw his right arm over his head and huddled facedown on the shoulder of the highway. Flaming debris showered from the air, littering the ground about him.

Then it was over. Walker rolled to his back, avoiding his throbbing shoulder, and pushed up. Flickering tongues of flame mingled with the churning clouds of oily, black smoke that covered car and squad vehicle. There was no movement around the fire. Walker shivered with a combination of relief and horror. Those inside had not escaped the trap he had set.

Slowly, he stood up. To his left, he found the rifle he had dropped in the fall, picked it up, and looked back at the two burning vehicles one last time. He turned and started quickly toward an embankment across the highway. The flames would be a beacon to any other of Gerald's ships in the area, and he was on foot again—although very much alive. He had to reach the cover of the houses and buildings south of the tollway before another of the shuttles came in search of him and their lost sister ship.

* * *

For fifteen minutes Walker sat on an overturned trash container inside a recessed doorway to a dentist's office in a shopping strip. Working and massaging the soreness from his left shoulder, he watched as the sun slowly crept into the sky, pushing back the predawn grays.

The golden light eased the tension from every muscle in his body. The way would be relatively easy now. Gerald was no fool. People still lived here near Chicago's city limits. He wouldn't risk a squad vehicle during the daylight. One unwanted glimpse of a shuttle and his closely guarded secret would be out.

Walker stood and rubbed at his eyes. If an attack came now, it would be from the ground. Gerald's toxin-immune shock troopers had miles of abandoned stores from which to select human clothing to replace their uniforms. And if he had found a car capable of starting, he was certain the Visitors could also.

"Speaking of cars," he said aloud, "it's time you found another one."

He glanced around and saw the tops of trees poking into the air behind the row of stores across the street from him. Trees rather than an orchard of neon signs was a good indication of a residential area. All he had to do was . . .

He caught himself. This wasn't Arlington Heights. There were people scattered throughout the area. The task of finding a car might not be as simple as he had first thought. He shrugged. He had no alternative but to try.

Lifting the rifle from where it leaned against the door, he stood and crossed the shopping center's parking lot. At the curb of a nameless four-lane street he paused, head turning both ways to check for nonexistent traffic.

"That's as far as I would go, if I were you, snake!"

Walker spun about and froze. He stared down the barrels of a 12-gauge shotgun!

Chapter Twelve

"Forget that damned rifle! Drop it! Drop it right now or kiss your belly good-bye 'cause you're not going to be wearing it much longer."

The muzzle of Walker's rifle dropped although his hands remained securely about the energy weapon. His gaze homed in on the barrels of the shotgun that stared at him over the top of the compact car parked in the lot. He couldn't get a good look at the man sighting down those twin barrels. Other than a bushy head of black hair, the man's face and head were hidden behind the gun.

"You heard him, lizard man!" Another male voice came from behind Walker, accompanied by the shuffle of two pairs of approaching feet.

"Snake? Lizard man? What the hell is going on here?" Walker started to turn when a pistol pressed to the back of his neck halted him.

"You were told to drop that rifle. I think you'd better do that right now," the man behind him said, punctuating his sentence with the metallic click of a pistol's hammer cocking.

Reluctantly Walker's hands uncurled from around the alien weapon. The rifle clanged to the street. Walker's stomach flip-flopped when he saw a young man no older than eighteen in black leather and chrome studs dart around him and scoop the rifle from the ground. The youth flashed a broad grin, minus one front tooth, as he pointed the weapon's muzzle at Walker.

"Okay, you slimy toad, hands on top of your head, fingers locked together," Missing Tooth ordered.

Walker complied. The pistol at his neck slid away, leaving a cool-feeling circle where the barrel had pressed against his skin.

"Damn! I hoped he'd put up a fight." The double-barreled shotgun eased from the roof of the compact. A young man perhaps a year or two older than Missing Tooth stepped from behind the car. "Thought I'd finally bagged me a lizard."

Like Missing Tooth, Double Barrel wore black leather pants that fit him like a second skin. About his waist was a broad belt with silver conchos. Spiked bands encircled his wrists. He wore yellow net for a shirt.

Walker's stomach did another sickening lurch. He had escaped Gerald's army of storm troopers only to fall into the hands of a street gang.

"You might still have a chance, Willie," the pistol-wielding man behind Walker replied. "Snakes are slippery. Always trying to get away. Are you going to make an escape, lizard man?"

Walker's eyes widened. The voice's owner stepped to his side. The man wore the starched blue uniform of Chicago's finest.

"Officer, what is going on here?" The policeman's appearance totally baffled Walker.

The instant Walker unlocked his fingers from on top his head, the policeman pressed the barrel of his service revolver to the tip of Walker's nose. The man thumbed back the hammer once again.

"Easy, lizard man, or I might cheat Willie out of his fun." The officer's narrowed eyes left no doubt that he was willing to pull the pistol's trigger. "Now, tell me what you and your Visitor friends were blowing up out there by the airport just before dawn."

"Visitor friends?" Walker sputtered. "What the hell are you talking about? My name's Sam Walker. I was—"

"He looks like a snake to me, Jim," Missing Tooth said to the policeman. "He's wearing a Visitor uniform and helmet. He was carrying a Visitor rifle. That makes him a Visitor."

Walker cringed inwardly. Those were practically the same words he had uttered to Paul Nordine when the resistance leader had asked if he was certain it had been Visitors who killed Kathleen.

"Look, I have to get into Chicago. I have to . . ." Walker tried to explain, but Officer Jim and Missing Tooth were listening to Double Barrel.

"Thing I don't understand is what's a snake doing here? The world's supposed to be poison to them." Double Barrel rubbed at his hairless chin. "And he doesn't talk like a snake."

Officer Jim edged back his hat, lowered his revolver, and eyed Walker skeptically. "Like Tommy said, he's in a shock trooper uniform, and he had a lizard rifle."

"There's one sure way to find out." Double-Barrel Willie stepped forward. Reaching out, he pinched Walker's cheek between thumb and forefinger and yanked.

"Dammit, man, that's real flesh and blood! Walker winced, unable to rub the pain from his cheek.

Unsatisfied Walker's face wasn't a Visitor mask, the youth in leather and net tried to rip away the opposite cheek.

He looked at the police officer and shrugged. "He isn't a snake, Jim."

"Then what the hell are you doing in that uniform?" The policeman glared at Walker, his tone doubly suspicious.

Walker spewed out his story as quickly and coherently as possible. The doubt in Officer Jim's dark eyes deepened. With a shake of his head, he reached up, took one of Walker's arms, and wrenched it to his back. Handcuffs snapped around Walker's right, then left wrist when the policeman jerked the other arm behind his prisoner.

"I think we'd better take this one to the station house, boys," Officer Jim said, shoving Walker forward. "The crew downtown can handle him in their own way."

Again Walker attempted to explain what had happened and the urgent need to contact Paul Nordine. For his trouble he received a stiff arm in the middle of his back and the order, "Keep walking, lizard lover."

The handcuffs came off Walker's wrists, and an arm shoved him into the open cell. The barred door slammed shut behind him.

Walker spun, hands grasping the steel bars. "Sergeant, you have to listen to me! Paul Nordine is in danger. Call resistance headquarters. Ask for Nordine or his second-in-command Steve Tyford. Both of them can identify me. They'll want to talk with me."

"Yeah, yeah." The overweight sergeant shook his head. "I might just do that, if the phone's working. Then again, I might forget, Walker, or whatever your snake name is. Just keep your shirt on. Things'll get done when they get done."

"Sergeant, can't I make you understand? Paul Nordine is in danger. The Visitors . . ." Walker slammed a palm against the bars when the man strode away without giving him so much as another glance.

To have made it this far and run smack into a man-made barrier. Walker pounded the bars again. He shouted, cursed, and eventually dropped to the edge of the mattress-less cot, holding his head in his hands. Two hours later the sergeant reappeared with a breakfast of two pieces of dry toast and a cup of coffee. This time the man only grunted in reply to Walker's pleas before walking away.

Alone in the four-cell holding room, Walker devoured the toast and coffee, realizing for the first time that days had passed since he had last eaten. He did the same with the lunch—toast, coffee, and a Snickers bar on the side—that the sergeant slipped through the bars after another six hours.

Walker was pacing his way back and forth along the cell's bars for what felt like the umpteen millionth time when the door leading to the main rooms of the police substation opened for the third time that day. The sergeant and three other officers entered, walking to the cell.

"Seems like they might have heard of you at resistance headquarters." The sergeant unlocked the door and slid it back. "These men have a car outside waiting to take you downtown."

Handcuffs were snapped back around Walker's wrists when he stepped from the cell. With an officer at each arm, he was escorted out the back of the substation. The "car" waiting for him was a blue and white paddy wagon. He managed to stumble inside to one of the shelflike seats running along the walls. One of the officers climbed in after him. Under the man's arm was Walker's Visitor helmet and rifle. Both were labeled with yellow evidence tags.

"Thought I was being taken to see Paul Nordine and not to trial," Walker said, tilting his head at the helmet and rifle.

The officer stared at him for several long, silent seconds, then glanced away without uttering a sound. He took a cigarette from a pack in his shirt pocket, lit it, and smoked as though he were alone in the paddy wagon.

Walker leaned back, adjusted his arms to the most comfortable position he could find, and waited. While the paddy wagon wasn't a chauffeured limousine and the officer wasn't the most congenial travel companion he had ever had the pleasure to meet, at least he was on the way into Chicago again. And that, after being locked behind bars all day, seemed like a major accomplishment!

Five cigarettes crushed beneath the sole of the officer's polished shoe later, the paddy wagon came to an abrupt halt. With a noncommittal grunt, the policeman picked up his evidence from the bench beside him, stood, and motioned Walker to the rear of the wagon. The two doors swung open. When Walker stepped down, he found he had once again grown two of Chicago's finest at his elbows.

Inside, the silent threesome led him to an empty room on the first floor of the Art Institute. There they waited for another hour without a word passing between them. Eventually the room's door opened, and Steven Tyford stepped through the doorway. All three officers jumped to their feet and did their imitation of coming to attention.

"Do you know this man, Mister Ty—" the cop who had ridden in the paddy wagon began.

Tyford cut him off. "Sam? What in hell are you doing in that uniform?" Before Walker could answer, Tyford's gaze shot to the officers. "And what do you mean bringing him in here like this! Get those handcuffs off. I told your captain that I knew this man."

"I guess that answers my question," the officer said while he removed the handcuffs. He then shoved the helmet and rifle into Walker's arms. "These belong to you. But I'd watch it. It isn't safe running around the city looking like a Visitor these days. Next time somebody might shoot first and ask questions later."

"Tell your captain that Mr. Nordine and I appreciate the police department's cooperation in this matter." Steve walked to the door and held it open until the three departed. When he looked at Walker, he said, "Sorry about keeping you so long, but we're in the process of moving headquarters. The city wants their art museum back. With luck, in another month or so there'll be no need for a headquarters or a resistance. Everything should be back to a semblance of normalcy."

He waved Walker to a chair and took a seat beside him. "Now tell me what's going on—and where is Janus?"

Walker shook his head. "I need to talk with Paul Nordine."

"I know, the police reported something about your saying Paul's life was in danger. Paul asked me to talk with you. He's in a meeting with several union officials at the moment, trying to get more food into the city. If necessary, you can talk with him after the meeting."

"Necessary!" Walker exploded. For an irrational moment he felt like throwing a fist into Tyford's face just to wake the man up. Instead he drew a deep breath to calm himself. He'd take the path of least resistance. "It started the night you and your men pulled out of Arlington Park . . ."

Slowly, detail by detail, Walker recounted the events of the past three days, beginning with the abduction and ending with Officer Jim and his two leather-clad joy boys. Steve's face was pale and his hands shaking when Walker concluded.

"Janus is dead?" he asked as though unable to accept the old man's murder.

Walker nodded. "This whole city might end up the same way unless something is done to stop Alicia."

Steve bit at his lower lip for a moment. "Look, Paul has to make this decision. I want you to stay right here. I'll get him to you as soon as I can, but it might take an hour or so to break him out of the meeting."

Walker glanced at a clock on the wall opposite him. It read seven in the evening. "I've been waiting all day," he said. "I can wait another hour."

Steve smiled. "We'll be back as soon as possible." He then rose and walked from the room.

Walker leaned back in the chair and rested his head against the wall. A sense of satisfaction suffused his body, edging away the weariness. He had made it, accomplished the task Jennifer and Janus had given their lives for. With a pleased smile lifting the corners of his mouth, he closed his eyes.

A shout in the hall brought Walker upright. He blinked and rubbed at his eyes. Two days on the run from Earth to the moon and back again, plus a day as a jailbird, had taken their toll. He had fallen asleep. He glanced at the clock on the wall.

Eight-thirty?

He rubbed his eyes again. The clock's hands didn't change. It was 8:30, and Steve and Paul were nowhere in sight.

Rising, he moved to the door, opened it, and glanced outside. Three men shouted at one another while they maneuvered dollies laden with file cabinets down the hallway. Walker called to them, "Any of you see Paul Nordine or Steve Tyford?"

"Sure. Both of them just went out that door." The nearest man nodded at the Institute's front door. "On their way to another of those meetings on the elections. Just a way to get out of all the hard work, if you ask me."

"Meeting?" Walker's head jerked to the door. "They were supposed to—"

He didn't finish the sentence. Shoving from the doorway, he ran from the building. Outside he saw Nordine and Tyford climbing into a dark blue sedan. He called, but the car doors shut. He wasted no more breath, but scrambled down the steps leading to the street two at a time.

With less than ten feet separating him from the vehicle, it peeled away from the curb. Walker stumbled to a halt. An icy finger tapped at the base of his spine. His gaze was riveted to the car's license plate—049-ESB!

Chapter Thirteen

049-ESB!

The horror anesthetizing Walker's brain dissipated. The treacherous, jagged pieces tumbled into place like a slow-motion film of a shattering mirror played backward. *Steven Tyford is Alicia's contact in Chicago!*

It all seemed so clear now. Steve was reluctant to leave his radio at Arlington Park because the radio was his link to the Mother Ship's commander. Walker had had the feeling that Gerald's men had known exactly where Janus and he were positioned the night of the abduction because they had! Steve had radioed the location of the stall to the waiting shuttles. The long wait in the Art Institute, Walker's inability to meet with Nordine were just delaying tactics to give Tyford time to get to Nordine.

Walker's anger burst forth in a spewing string of curses. He'd lay odds that Steve was also responsible for the day he spent in the substation's cell. With him neatly locked away on the edge of Chicago, Tyford had had time to scheme, to formulate a plan to abduct Nordine and take him to Gerald's waiting shuttles.

Convert or traitor? Walker wasn't certain. And at the moment it didn't matter. The results would be the same. Nordine would be placed on a squad vehicle and four hours later, he would be introduced to the terrors of Alicia's conversion chamber.

Walker spun about, running back to the Art Institute. The resistance, the police had to be told, warned of Alicia's ploy to reconquer the city she had lost less than two weeks ago. An icy band tightened about Walker's chest when he wrenched the Institute's door open.

Who do I tell? Nordine and Tyford were the only ones who knew him within the resistance. And who in either the resistance or police would believe the outrageous tale that Paul Nordine had been kidnapped by his trusted second-in-command, who intended to place him in the hands of Earth's would-be conquerors? Conquerors who could not return to this world because of a toxin that had made the atmosphere poisonous to their reptilian bodies.

Who will even listen to a man dressed in a shock trooper uniform? Walker's stomach sank, his gut knotted. The absurd simplicity of Alicia's plan stacked the cards against him. No one would listen to him. No one would believe Steve was capable of harming the man he had so loyally served during the long fight against the Visitors.

There was only one man who understood, who grasped the treachery weaving through Chicago. That man was Samuel Walker.

In your hands, Jennifer's and Janus's voices echoed in his head. If Steve was to be stopped, he had to do it himself.

Walker's head jerked around. His gaze searched and found what he was looking for.

In the Institute's parking lot sat a white pickup truck. Its long bed was half filled with the filing cabinets the three men in the hall had been removing from the museum. The door to the truck stood open. Walker couldn't see whether the keys were in the ignition. It didn't matter. He was quite capable of hot-wiring the vehicle.

Tugging open the door to the Institute, he sprinted down the hall to the room in which Steve had so easily waylaid him. Snatching up the helmet and rifle, he ran back to the front door.

Outside, the three workers rolled their laden dollies into the back of the pickup. Walker contained his impatience while the men unloaded their burdens by peeling away the yellow police-evidence labels on the side of the helmet and rifle butt. By the time the last trace of the sticky tags was gone, so were the three men.

Walker hastened down the steps to the Institute, then ran to the parking lot. He smiled when he slid behind the steering wheel. The truck's keys lay nestled in a plastic tray attached to the top of the dashboard. Slamming the driver's door, he inserted the key, pumped the gas twice, and twisted the key. The engine caught.

Filing cabinets rattled, bounced, then tumbled from the back of the truck, scattering their reams of records across the parking lot as Walker peeled away. He didn't look back at the mess he had caused. His attention focused on the night-darkened streets of a Visitor-crippled Chicago.

Walker cut the lights to the pickup the moment he passed under the O'Hare interchanges and sped west on the Northwest Tollway. A half-moon provided all the illumination he needed to avoid the occasional skeleton of a car or a truck littering the multilane highway.

He realized that the same moon reflected off the white surface of the truck, making him an easy target for any squad vehicle Gerald might have scouting the area. There was nothing he could do about that except keep his fingers crossed and hope Gerald and his shock troopers were too wrapped up in their preparations for Nordine's arrival to worry about a lone truck on the highway.

Luck was with him. Following the highway signs pointing the way to Arlington Park, he exited from the tollway to the west of the racetrack. The highway, which had once funneled traffic into one of the track's main entrances, curved around the western boundary of the stable area.

For an instant Walker considered floorboarding the truck and plowing through the locked gate. He grimaced. The entrance would be dramatic enough for the climactic conclusion of a Hollywood chase scene. Hero at the wheel of his trusty truck would roar into the track with villains scrambling away on each side. Screeching to a halt before the kidnap victim, the hero would throw open a door, save the victim, and peel away as credits rolled across the screen.

Lucky hero, he thought. A pat script and tight directing paved the way for such a daring rescue. Trouble was, this wasn't a movie script, and the lizards within the track weren't extras hired to play the part of awkward, bumbling heavies.

If Walker slammed through the gate, two hundred energy rifles would be trained on the pickup. He'd be lucky to make it halfway to the barns before the truck and he went up in a ball of flame. And even if he somehow managed to get through the barrage of energy bolts, he still had to find Nordine.

Walker glanced at the helmet lying beside him on the seat. The uniform, rifle, and helmet had been enough to fool the guards on the Mother Ship. They would now be his ticket through Gerald's ranks—if his luck held out.

Following the road a half mile west of the track's stable area, Walker swung down an exit ramp and cut the engine. The truck traveled for another eighth of a mile before rolling to a halt.

Walker sucked at his cheeks. He would like to have the truck closer to the track, but he couldn't risk the sound of the motor. Besides, he tried to reassure himself, if he was able to get to Nordine, he had no guarantee they would leave the track by the same path he entered.

If I can get to Nordine. He left the keys in the ignition, opened the door, and stepped into the night. *If I can get into the track without being noticed.*

Running east two blocks down residential streets, he reached a dead end. A wide field covered with waist-high weeds and the chain-link fence enclosing the track were all that separated him from the stable area. In a crouch, Walker entered the field and rushed forward.

Again luck rode with him. He reached the fence without glimpsing a guard. He stood and reached for a hold above his head in the chain-link barrier. And he froze.

The crunch of sand and gravel beneath booted feet came from his left. Two shock troopers, rifles in hand, stepped from the side of a barn and walked along the fence.

Walker leaped back and dropped facedown in the high weeds. He turned the muzzle of his rifle toward the fence. His finger curled around the trigger.

The footsteps grew closer. Through the stand of weeds he saw the dark silhouettes of the approaching guards. He heard their whispered voices—a male and a female— discussing the possible promotions in store for those under Gerald's command if their mission succeeded.

They passed by him without so much as a glance to the west.

Walker released a long-held breath in a soft sigh when they reached the end of the line of barns and turned east. He pushed to a crouch again as they disappeared behind the barns, and listened. Only when he no longer even imagined their footsteps did he stand, sling the rifle over a shoulder, scramble up the fence, and drop to the other side.

Head jerking from side to side, he double-checked to make certain he hadn't been discovered. The dual headlights of an approaching car glared from the west. Walker darted into the shadows of the nearest stable and watched.

The car approached the entrance to the stable area. Halting at the fence, the driver waited until a shock trooper stepped from a security booth and edged open the gate.

Walker's mind raced too fast for him to consider what would have happened had that guard seen him on the fence. More important was the car. He was too far away to see the occupants, but he had no doubt that the man behind the steering wheel was Steve Tyford. Nordine's second-in-command had apparently taken the longer, more concealed route through the deserted suburbs to reach the racetrack.

When the car trundled into the stable area, Walker darted around the barn, left the protection of the shedrow's shadows, and ran to the next stable in the long row that stretched toward the main racecourse. Five barns to the east, he halted. Three shock troopers walked between the stables.

For a moment Walker considered stepping out and testing his disguise. He shoved the idea aside. He was still too close to the fringes of the stable area. Soldiers stationed this far from the parking lot used to land the shuttle craft were surely guards. To risk confrontation would be stupid, if not suicidal.

Waiting until the three passed, Walker slipped from the veiling shadows and hurried down the row of barns. Five stables from the barn fronting the parking lot, he found it impossible to continue without risking detection. The area was swarming with shock troopers in red uniforms.

Flipping down the smoky faceplate to his helmet, Walker gave his eyes a minute to adjust to the dimness, sucked down a steadying breath, and stepped into the open. He smiled. No head turned to him nor did a reverberating voice question his presence.

So far so good, Walker, he silently congratulated himself while he hastened past the remaining four barns and entered the shedrow of the last stable in the row. There he saw a ring of twenty soldiers milling about Tyford's dark blue car. To the left of the circle, Steve and Gerald, eyes hidden behind dark sunglasses, stood talking. Moonlight bathed the white form of a shuttle poised at the center of the parking lot. Its side door lay open and waiting.

Paul Nordine was nowhere in sight.

Drawing another breath, Walker strode from the last barn and casually walked to the shock troopers encircling Tyford's sedan. He found Nordine.

The Chicago resistance leader sat upright in the front seat of the car—or was propped there. The man's head lay on his right shoulder, and his eyes were closed as though in sleep. Drugged or unconscious, Walker couldn't be certain. Either way, Nordine was in no condition to travel. Even if he were, Walker would have had to find a way to get to the man.

Walker's gaze ran over the interior of the car. His pulse doubled its tempo. The keys were in the ignition. If he could get to the driver's side and slip behind the wheel, there might be a chance at escape. A slim chance, he realized, but a chance.

Edging around the circle of shock troopers who peered into the car or talked among themselves, Walker maneuvered to the driver's side of the sedan. A soldier who was boasting of his sexual conquests to a companion beside him, shifted his position. Walker slipped next to the car. His hand was now only three inches from the door handle.

Mentally, he outlined his plan of action. Shove the braggart aside, open the door, jump in, start the car, then floorboard it. He'd worry about the energy rifles, gates, and the shuttle chase that would surely follow when they presented themselves.

The first item on his agenda was getting into the car. Walker turned to face the bragging soldier's back, ready to push him away from the door.

"Get Nordine into the squad vehicle," Gerald hissed out to the soldiers. "Sergeant, get your men loaded. Alicia is waiting for us."

On the opposite side of the car, one of the shock troopers opened the passenger door. Two of the soldiers lifted Nordine's unmoving body and carried him toward the shuttle.

"You heard the high captain." A hand shoved Walker's back. "Move out."

Uncertain what else to do, Walker fell in rank and marched aboard the waiting craft. Ten minutes later he stood within the shuttle shoulder to shoulder with twenty shock troopers as they hurtled through space toward Earth's moon.

Chapter Fourteen

A squad vehicle was never designed for interplanetary flight, either that or the ability of the average Visitor to endure discomfort far exceeded that of the average human being. This was what Walker decided after standing a quarter of the way to the far side of the moon.

Neither bench nor chair nor seating shelf lined the shuttle's walls. There was nothing Walker could do except stand, unless he wanted to give away his charade. So he stood, making certain he didn't lock his knees—the last thing he needed to do was pass out—while continuing to worry.

He worried about one of the shock troopers speaking to him. But no one did. They just stood and faced forward, staring at each other across the shuttle.

He worried about sweat, his own. Three days had passed since Janus and he had been abducted, three days without a bath. Surely the Visitors could smell him, could notice that a mammal was among their number. They didn't; they stood facing forward and stared at one another.

He worried about escaping from the Mother Ship for a

second time. If he could somehow manage to free Paul Nordine and get inside a shuttle, he still had to pilot the craft back to Earth. While Jennifer had taught him the controls, soloing an alien ship would be a far cry from testing the controls with an accomplished pilot looking over his shoulder.

His last worry kept his mind and eyes occupied for the remainder of the flight. With the dark faceplate shielding his face, he could keep his head positioned straight ahead while shifting his eyes to the side without being noticed. That sideways glance gave him an excellent view of the control console and the pilot's hands. Each jab of a finger, each flick of a switch, each nudge of a lever provided the opportunity for him to review all that Jennifer had taught.

By the time the squad vehicle slipped behind the moon and the fleet of Visitor Mother Ships loomed ahead, Walker was certain he could fly one of the compact vehicles—if he and Nordine could get to one.

Outside the shuttle the monstrous bodies of the great Mother Ships slipped by. Unlike Walker's first arrival on Alicia's city-sized craft, the space around the ships was filled with activity. Squad vehicles darted back and forth between the vessels like bees flitting about hives.

"Why all the activity?" Gerald spoke to the pilot.

"Alicia revealed her plans for the Chicago conversion to the rest of the Mother Ships' commanders this morning," the nameless pilot replied. "The official comings and goings haven't stopped since. Every Mother Ship commander had decided that he or she must meet privately with Alicia."

"They maneuver for favorable positions," Gerald replied. "When we succeed, they all want to stand at Alicia's right arm. They know Our Great Leader will be displeased with their inactivity since the toxin was introduced into Earth's atmosphere. Only Alicia attempts to open a way for our return. They realize that she will rise to command the whole fleet."

Walker tuned the two out, his gaze returning to the fleet. For the first time he noticed the open bays on all the ships. An idea wedged into his mind. The unusual shuttle traffic would be to his advantage. *When* (he forced himself to think in the positive) Nordine and he made it into a squad vehicle, the bay would lay open and unobstructed for their escape.

He saw rather than felt the shuttle nose about and align itself with the gaping mouth of a bay in the underside of a Mother Ship. The pilot eased back the control levers on both sides of his couch. The squad vehicle slipped through the open port. Inside, the craft hovered, turned, then floated across the white landing bay to a red bull's-eye stenciled on the floor.

A slight jar ran through the soles of Walker's feet when the ship touched down. His gaze shot back to the pilot's hands. A single red button high on the left side of the console opened the shuttle's side door. Another three red buttons in front of the pilot's couch went green when the Visitor pressed them. The shuttle's power shut down.

Any further information he might have gleaned from watching the extraterrestrial pilot's movements had to be abandoned. The shock trooper sergeant near the door ordered his squad from the vessel. In step with his unearthly companions, Walker marched from the ship and stood at attention in the landing bay.

A moment later Gerald walked out of the shuttle. Behind him came Paul Nordine with a shock trooper locked on each of his arms. The Chicago resistance leader appeared dazed and confused. His eyes were wild and dilated, the eyes of a man fighting the effect of a drug.

"You and you, take the lead." The sergeant pointed to two of the soldiers, who fell in ahead of Nordine and his escorts. "You and you."

Walker's runaway pulse drowned the rest of the sergeant's

order. The sergeant pointed at him! Swallowing, Walker and the shock trooper at his side stepped behind Nordine and his two guards. As Gerald, followed by his prisoner and six escorts, passed through the angular doorway into the Mother Ship's interior dimness, Walker allowed himself one soft sigh. At least he knew this routine from his own experience.

Unlike his first visit to the Mother Ship, his head was clear, his thinking focused. He carefully filed away each corridor they marched down and noted each turn made, committing the way back to the landing bay to memory.

Eventually the procession reached the conversion chamber. Alicia and her four white-smocked assistants waited at the control console. Nordine, still rocky from whatever Tyford had used on him, did little more than moan a few grunts of protests when two of the shock troopers stripped him and led him into the glass cage.

Imitating the action of the other shock troopers, Walker backed to a wall and stood at attention. He closed his eyes and retraced his mental map of the route back to the shuttles. But no matter how hard he concentrated, he could not block out the anguish of Paul's screams.

A straight two hundred feet from the conversion chamber and a dog leg to the left brought the five guards and one shock-trooper-disguised human being to the cell. Walker watched carefully while the lead soldier's fingers ran over the panel of buttons inset on the wall beside the door, memorizing the pattern.

As the four carrying Nordine entered the cell to drop him on a cot, the trooper who marched at Walker's side stepped to the right of the open door and unslung his rifle. Walker followed suit, positioning himself to the left of the door.

"Richard and I will be back to relieve you in an hour," one of the shock troopers said, glancing at Walker and his partner. "I'd stay on my toes if I were you. You know what happened to Dan and Joyce when they let Alicia's last two guests escape."

Walker nodded, but the guard on the other side of the door spoke in a female voice: "Dan couldn't think straight. He'd been trying to get into Jennifer's bed for months. You don't have to worry about that with me, Wesley."

Wesley chuckled. "No man has to worry about you, Belinda. However, if your partner were female, I would worry."

Belinda's grip tightened about her rifle when Wesley and the other three guards turned and strode away to disappear around the bend in the corridor. "Bastard! Just because I wouldn't bundle with him, he thinks I prefer other women!"

Walker said nothing. He was trying to convince himself that in spite of the voice he heard that it wasn't a woman beneath the uniform and helmet, that Belinda was a reptilian creature from another star system come to conquer his world, that what he had to do was necessary to save Paul Nordine—and himself.

Belinda turned and stared at him. "You don't talk much, do you? What's the matter?"

Walker didn't give her the opportunity to complete the second question. Stepping forward, he swung the butt upward, ramming it beneath the lower edge of the woman's faceplate. It was the same tactic he had seen Jennifer use on the shuttle guard during their escape from Alicia's Mother Ship. It was just as effective on Belinda as it had been on the guard.

A solid crack resounded through the corridor when the rifle's stock met the woman's chin. With a surprised grunt-groan, Belinda dropped to the floor and lay there unmoving. Walker stood above her a moment, afraid to check if she was unconscious or dead. He didn't want to know.

Turning from the crumpled woman, he stared at the panel

of buttons, sucked at his teeth, then pressed the one on the upper left corner, followed by the one on the lower right. His finger finally moved across the center row from left to right.

The cell door hissed opened. Inside, Paul pushed from the cot on his wobbling elbows. "Not again. Not so soon!"

Walker shoved up his faceplate and grinned at the resistance leader. "I'm not the calvary, but I'm afraid that I'm all you're going to get."

"Wal—Walker?" Nordine's face twisted with doubt and confusion. "Sam Walker?"

"One and the same." Walker hauled Belinda into the cell. "Her uniform might be a little tight, but it's the best I could do. Get into it. We haven't that much time. Two more of her playmates are due back here in less than an hour."

"How—how did you get here?" Nordine's words were slurred and uncertain.

Not waiting for Nordine, Walker gave an abbreviated version of what had occurred as he stooped and began to strip away Belinda's red uniform. The human disguise beneath was complete and quite convincing.

"Then you know about Steve?" Paul asked when Walker concluded.

"Janus and I were supposed to help him." Walker stared down at the nude woman while Paul managed to work legs, then arms into the jumpsuit-like uniform.

Belinda was a human; she had to be. Walker couldn't convince himself that a lizard lay hidden beneath the attractive form of the small-breasted woman at his feet. He stooped again and brushed a fingertip over her cheek. The skin was so cool to his touch. He pinched the cheek and jerked.

The flesh-imitating makeup resisted for an instant, then tore away. Green scales mottled by black lay beneath. His stomach churning, Walker rose and looked away.

"Care to do the same thing to your own cheek?" Paul stood, the muzzle of Belinda's rifle aimed directly at Walker's stomach.

Walker shrugged, remembering his own caution when Jennifer had appeared in the cell. He reached up, pinched his cheek, yanked, and winced. "Satisfied?"

"Satisfied." Paul grinned. "Now, how do we get out of here?"

"Faceplate down," Walker answered. He snapped his own faceplate into place. "Follow me and do exactly what I do. And remember, whatever happens don't speak."

Paul lowered his faceplate and nodded without uttering a sound to confirm he understood. Walker nodded in reply before stepping from the cell with Paul on his heels. Reversing the button-pressing pattern was all it took to close the cell on Belinda's marred beauty.

As much as Walker wished he could disappear into the maintenance shafts Jennifer had led Janus and him through, he knew only one route to the landing bay. That was the one he had taken. With Paul a step behind him, he moved down the corridor, passed the unguarded door to the conversion chamber, and went out into the maze of tunnels and corridors riddling the Mother Ship.

A half hour later the two men reached the exit that opened on the landing bay. Inside, the wide port lay open, revealing the blackness of space beyond. However, escape to the freedom outside the port would be a trick. Workers and guards scurried here and there around the bay.

Walker's gaze centered on a craft a hundred feet to the right of the bay's entrance. The ship's nose resembled a shuttle, but it was no more than half the size of a squad vehicle. *Fighter,* flitted through Walker's mind. The craft had the sleek design of a military ship built for action. Its side door also lay open and unguarded.

Tilting his head to the ship, Walker stepped into the

landing bay with Paul at his side. Those hundred feet were like an equal number of miles to the former helicopter pilot. He had to force himself to remain calm, stop his feet from making a mad dash to the waiting ship, had to present the image that he belonged here and knew exactly what he was doing.

The charade worked. They crossed to the ship and marched inside without drawing a passing glance. Snatching off his helmet, Walker rushed to the control console and pushed the red button at the upper left-hand corner. The side door closed.

Only then did Walker allow himself the leisure to study the craft's interior. A tail gunner's seat and dual energy cannons at the rear of the ship confirmed his earlier guess about the craft's nature. It was a fighter of some type.

"Can you fly this thing?" Paul arched an eyebrow.

"That's what we're about to find out." Tossing aside rifle and helmet, Walker slid into the pilot's couch. He motioned Paul to the seat beside him, then reached for the row of green buttons directly before him on the console. "Here goes nothing."

He tapped the buttons, bringing them to a glowing red life. The constant ache of Walker's teeth increased as the ship's drive came alive.

Walker smiled. He reached down and grasped the control levers on each side of the couch and eased them forward. Simultaneously the craft lifted from the floor of the landing bay and nosed toward the open port. Outside, heads of guards and workers jerked about.

Too late! Walker laughed aloud, thrusting the levers forward even more.

The trim, compact Visitor fighter responded to his command and shot from the bay into the void of space.

Chapter Fifteen

Walker had once read that gravity was the weakest force in the universe. At the moment, it felt like an invisible fist that had closed about the fighter, tugging it toward the slim silvery crescent to the left. Jennifer had made the flight around the moon seem so simple, while he had to constantly struggle with the control levers to keep the blip of light on the minidisplay screen on something resembling a straight line.

"The guns appear easy enough to operate," Paul's voice intruded on Walker's string of mental curses. "There's a button on each arm that's a firing mechanism. The barrels are stationary, but there's some type of electronic sight that—"

"Good." Walker watched the blip slide closer to the semicircle representing the moon on the display. "Damn!"

He shifted the levers to counteract the fingers of gravity that pulled them down. The Visitor fighter slipped back on course, remained there a second or two until it started to ease back toward the moon. Walker corrected the course again.

"Anything wrong?" Paul's forehead wrinkled with concern while he lowered himself into the couch beside Walker.

"Nothing a degree in astrophysics wouldn't help." Walker grunted. "And I thought the air traffic around Los Angeles was bad. Never tried dodging a moon before."

The screen displayed the ship sliding back on course when he adjusted the controls once again. Walker's eyes narrowed. Three blips that weren't there a second ago blinked at the lower edge of the screen.

Easing the controls to the right, he watched those three blips shift with him. He slipped to the left. The blips followed—and inched closer.

"Paul, I hope you're right about being able to operate those tail guns." Walker glanced at the man beside him. "We've got company. Three ships moving up behind us like bats out of hell."

Paul studied the display screen, shoved from the couch, and hastened to the tail guns. "I can't see them, but I've got three targets on the sight."

"The top of the sight is twelve o'clock, the right edge three o'clock," Walker called back to the resistance leader. "Where are the three ships?"

"Six o'clock!"

Walker eased forward on what he had designated as the altitude lever. The nose of the craft dipped in relation to the moon's widening crescent on his left. He realized there were no ups and downs in space, not in the usual earthbound sense. But to think in the terms he was accustomed to made things a damned sight easier for his mind to comprehend.

"Six o'clock, just south of my cross hairs," Paul's voice echoed from the rear of the craft.

Walker eased the lever down a bit.

"That's it. That's it," Paul said. "Just a bit more and the middle one will be dead center of the sight."

Walker gave him the bit more he asked for, then leveled

when the blip centered on Paul's cross hairs. There was no sizzle of energy bolts, no jarring vibrations that ran through the ship. Only the slight click of thumbs on firing buttons sounded in the fighter while Paul unleashed a stream of blue bursts into the blackness of space.

Walker watched his minidisplay as he pulled back on the lever and shifted back on course. The three blips remained on the screen.

"They could be out of range," Paul said.

"Which means we are too," Walker replied. "And as far as I'm concerned—"

"Son of a bitch!" Paul cried out. "I got one! I got one!"

Walker's eyes rolled to the minidisplay. Only two blips lit the screen where there had been three only seconds ago. The smile that started to form on Walker's lips faded.

"Sam, the bastards are firing on us!" Paul's voice tightened.

Walker didn't need to turn. He saw six streams of pulse-burst energy shoot beneath them and glide harmlessly into space. In an instant he realized that Paul's shot had been a matter of luck. The ships behind them obviously had their own sights and had only been waiting for the fugitives' craft to drop into their cross hairs. Walker's course adjustment had accidentally saved them from being instantaneously converted into cosmic debris.

The Visitors hadn't expected an attack from the escaping ship. They had been caught off guard and had lost a ship for their carelessness. They wouldn't be careless again.

"I want to know everything they're doing back there, Paul," Walker called out. "The instant their positions shift I want to know!"

"Eight o'clock creeping to the center of the sight," Paul answered.

Walker tugged back on the control lever.

"Seven o'clock, bottom of sight."

Walker licked at his dry lips. His gaze lifted to the wide viewport stretched across the nose of the fighter. The moon's crescent had disappeared behind the ship. The Earth, blue marbled with white, loomed ahead.

"Seven o'clock, shifting toward center," Paul called out again.

Four hours. Walker worked the control levers again. *Four hours and over a quarter of a million miles.* It was a long way home for a chopper pilot trying to play astronaut at the controls of an alien ship.

"Delay?" Lewis, the commander of the Houston Mother Ship, asked coolly when Alicia waved the messenger from her private quarters.

"A temporary delay, Lewis." Alicia repressed the anger that threatened to destroy her calm exterior. "Paul Nordine has managed to escape my ship."

"Escape! You call that a temporary delay, Alicia?" Lewis pushed upright in his chair and stared at the woman.

"I have three ships in pursuit," Alicia lied. The messenger had told her about the destruction of one of the shuttles. "Nordine will have to be eliminated, of course. But there are others in Chicago who will serve our purpose just as well. It's only a matter of contacting the convert Steven Tyford and giving him another target. Nordine is an inconvenience at worst."

"*Our* purpose, Alicia, or *yours*?" Lewis stood and shook his head. "The other commanders will not view this favorably."

Alicia wanted to tell the heavyset man what he and the rest of the Mother Ship commanders could do with their views. Only she had acted while the rest of them cowered behind Earth's moon, afraid to even contact their home world and report their failure to the Great Leader. Alicia contained the sharpness of her tongue. When she spoke there was no change in her tone.

"And you, Lewis, how do you view the situation?"

The Houston Mother Ship commander took a deep breath. "I make no judgment. The Chicago conversion is your plan. I am willing to watch and allow you to handle it."

How generous! Contempt seeped through Alicia's every thought. Lewis had just politely told her that she had made her own bed and now had to lie in it.

"Your plan was basically sound, Alicia. But there are those among our rank who believe you should have consulted with the other commanders before implementing it," Lewis continued.

Had she done that, Gerald and his toxin-immune troops would have been yanked from her command. Couldn't they see that there was only one key to Earth's conquest, and only one hand at a time could hold and turn that key?

"I acted only for the glory of Our Great Leader," she replied, her tone more defensive than she desired.

"We all live to serve Our Great Leader, Alicia," Lewis replied. "There are those who think that you have attempted to deny them their chance to serve."

"That was never my intention," Alicia said, adding a note of wounded shock to her voice. *Although you cold meat eaters would have robbed me, given the chance!* Like it or not, she had to placate the other commanders, allow them to save face without letting them interfere with her plans. "Yet I can see how my actions could be misconstrued. Perhaps if an advisory council of the Mother Ship commanders were convened . . ."

"A wise move, Commander Alicia." Lewis grinned and nodded his approval. "While all the commanders could not serve, we could elect, say, five to represent the fleet. And of course it would be preferable if the council convened on your ship until this temporary delay has been overcome."

"Of course." Alicia flashed her fellow commander her warmest smile. The last thing she wanted was Lewis and his interfering council aboard her vessel, but for the time being she could endure their presence. It was simply a matter of diplomacy. Later, when she had succeeded, she would see that Lewis and the others paid dearly for this intrusion.

Four hours later, Lewis and four other commanders entered the control room of Alicia's ship to await word on the destruction of the stolen ship containing Paul Nordine.

Russia, China, Japan, the Pacific Ocean rushed by in a streaked blur of colors that were swallowed in the inky darkness of night. Walker nosed the fighter into the atmosphere. He whispered a prayer that Jennifer had been right—that the onboard computer would prevent him from transforming the ship into a flaming cinder.

"They're still riding our tail," Paul shouted from the rear of the fighter. "Twelve o'clock, top of the sight."

"Bastards!" Walker had hoped he would lose the two pursuit ships the moment they entered Earth's atmosphere.

He pushed the altitude-control lever down. The craft nosed through a thin layer of wispy clouds. Ahead night gave way to a purple-gray predawn sky, then to the blue of morning. The console's minidisplay was no longer illuminated with a circle representing Earth, but provided a detailed map of the terrain they sailed over. Walker smiled. A Rand McNally road atlas couldn't have been better than the computer display. He now shot across the Rockies and above the Colorado plains.

Better than knowing their exact location was the fact that he was in the atmosphere. He might not be a jet jockey, but this was air, real air, and it was his home ground, his ball park.

"Twelve o'clock drifting to center." Paul reported a shift in the two ships' position.

"I'm going to pull up, then dive," Walker answered. "That will give you a chance at laying two lines of fire across their noses."

Not waiting for a reply, Walker tugged the control lever back. The ship shot upward. The click of Paul's thumbs on the firing buttons accompanied by the exploding crackle of energy bolts came from the rear of the ship. Walker shoved the lever down. Paul's thumbs and the sizzle of blasts spoke again.

"Still on us," Paul said.

The two blips trailing them on the computer's map gave testimony to the failure of the maneuver. The map also indicated they had crossed into Kansas. Walker could only guess at the mach speed of the craft. A shiver crept up his spine at the tally that rolled into his head. He pushed it aside. If the fighter could make it from the moon to the Earth in four hours, it could withstand the speed he now pushed it to.

"Twelve o'clock sinking toward center."

Reacting to Paul's report, Walker dived. To the left on the horizon, rolling gray thunderclouds loomed like mountains in the sky. Walker banked and shot into the storm front.

The two trailing blips blinked from the computer display.

"What the hell?" Paul's surprise equalled his companion's. "They've disappeared. What's going on?"

"I don't know." Walker couldn't figure it out. One moment the ships were there and in the next gone. "Maybe we've got an instrument failure. Keep your eyes peeled."

If it were an instrument glitch, the display map didn't falter. It faithfully tracked the terrain below, showing their course across Kansas and Missouri. When they crossed the border into Illinois, Walker swung the fighter north toward Chicago and eased back on the drive control to slow their speed. This close he didn't want to overshoot their destination.

"Still nothing," Paul announced. "It looks like muddy soup outside. How far do these clouds go?"

"I don't know." Walker's jaw sagged when he glanced at the display.

The storm front wasn't indicated anywhere on the instruments. It was as though the Visitors' scanners were blind to the clouds.

A smile that grew to a grin spread across his face. That was it! The scanners were blind to the clouds. They had to be. The Visitors came from a water-poor planet. Large accumulations of water vapor in the air were probably unknown to them. The scanners didn't know how to deal with the clouds, thus they ignored them. In doing so, the scanners of the pursuit ships had lost their quarry!

"We've done it!" Walker laughed while he quickly outlined his theory to Paul. "I'm going to set this baby right down in the Art Institute's parking lot."

Slowing the ship's speed, Walker dropped altitude again. Chicago appeared at the top of the display screen. He began a gliding descent toward the city. In another ten minutes, they'd be home free.

Ahead the clouds thinned. Patches of sunlight poked through here and there. Then the thunderheads vanished. The ship shot into clear, unobscured air.

Walker saw the blips on the display and heard Paul's voice at the same time.

"Sam, they're sitting on our tails!"

Bolts of blue—four streaming trails of pulse-beam energy—shot by the fighter from stern to nose.

Walker reacted rather than thought. He wrenched back on the altitude lever. The fighter's nose jerked up.

For the first time in an alien craft, Walker felt the g pull. The onboard computer protected the ship from exceeding its structural limitations. However, it did not protect its human pilot. Six, eight g's slammed Walker into the couch's padding. He screamed through clenched teeth, fighting off the invisible force that tried to drag him into unconsciousness as he maneuvered the fighter in a tight loop.

Up, over, and level. Then he was sitting on the tails of the two Visitor craft. The pursued became the pursuer. His thumbs found the firing buttons atop the control levers and depressed them while he slipped directly behind the ship to his right.

Both Visitor fighters banked in opposite directions. The evasive action came a split second too late for the craft Walker homed in on. A burst of blue blasted directly between the dark circles marking its rear cannons.

The blue-white of the energy bolt was lost in flaring flames of orange and yellow. The Visitor craft no longer flew but tumbled wildly through the air on an arching course that ended in a flash of white and a cloud of greasy smoke when the ship plummeted into the ground.

Walker didn't have to search for the remaining ship. The stream of its energy bursts came from directly ahead. While he had eliminated one ship, the other had circled and rushed at him in a head-on attack.

Again there was no time for thought. Walker's arms eased the directional lever from side to side while his thumbs kept the firing buttons depressed.

The last of the three pursuit ships vanished in a blinding flash of white as one of Walker's bursts struck home.

"Got the son of a—"

Walker's victory grin evaporated. Debris from the exploding ship hurtled through the air and slammed into the side of the fighter. The control levers wrenched from Walker's hands.

Spinning, the fighter hurled out of control toward Chicago's spires rising below.

Chapter Sixteen

"Withdraw your forces, Alicia." Ian's voice broke the silence that had hung in the Mother Ship's control room since communication with the last pursuit ship had died in a burst of crackling static. "The human has destroyed your ships. You have no choice but to withdraw the troops from the deserted racetrack."

Alicia's aquamarine eyes turned their glare on the commander of the London Mother Ship. Anger constricted her throat as she held back the curses she wanted to spit into the faces of the five who had come aboard her ship to judge her.

"Ian is right." This from overweight Lewis. "We can't afford to lose the immune shock troopers at the outpost. While your scientists have been unable to duplicate the antitoxin in their systems, those men are still our only key to defeating the poison the humans use against us. With all our scientists working together, we have a chance at developing our own antitoxin."

"Withdraw your troops, Alicia." Maria, commander of the Mexico City Mother Ship, added her vote. "Our Great

Leader cannot afford to lose those men. Your plan is still basically solid. With the advice of the other commanders, we can select another city in which to implement it, one where they have not been alerted to our presence."

It was slipping between her fingers. Alicia felt all her plans wriggle away, eluding her. Failure weighted her shoulders as she nodded, acquiescing to their decision.

"High Captain Gerald and five shuttles will be dispatched to Earth immediately." Her tone was one of defeat. "He will oversee the evacuation of the troops and the equipment at the outpost."

Alicia's gaze avoided their gloating smiles when she turned to summon Gerald to the control room.

Walker's hands groped and found the control levers on each side of his couch. He fought the panic that welled in his chest and sought to rob him of the last vestiges of rational thought.

Break the spin, then pull out! he ordered himself. *Break the spin!*

He felt the ship, sensed the rolling rhythm as it spun downward. Gradually he pulled the directional lever toward him. The spin slowed and stopped. Behind him, he heard Paul Nordine moan gratefully.

Walker did not allow himself the luxury of a smile. He still had to pull the ship up or abruptly end their flight by splattering them in the center of Chicago's Loop.

He tugged the altitude control back.

Nothing!

The ship did not respond. It plunged head-on toward the buildings below!

Walker thrust the lever full forward. The fighter's angle of descent remained unchanged. Whatever had slammed into the small craft had severed a portion of the ship's electronic nerve system. Exactly what, he wasn't certain. All he knew was that without altitude control, the ship that had carried them safely from the moon to the Earth had now become their coffin.

Walker yanked back on the lever. Something caught. Vibrations ran through the ship. The craft's nose inched up.

Vibrations transformed into quivers and from quivers to tremors. The fighter groaned, the protest of metal strained to its limit. The ship quaked as though attempting to shake itself apart.

Still Walker pulled back on the control lever, fighting the force that tried to jerk it from his grip. The ship's blunt snout crept ever higher.

Not enough, dammit! Walker tapped the directional control. The fighter slid to one side, then to the other. He corrected and overcorrected before he aligned the craft with an east-west ribbon of war-torn concrete—the remnants of Chicago's Eisenhower Expressway.

The ship bucked and wrenched, and the nose jerked up— and still the fighter sank into the canyon of skyscrapers at Chicago's heart. Beneath the fighter Eisenhower became Congress Parkway. The ship skimmed over the treetops of Grant Park, over Buckingham Fountain, across Lake Shore Drive. Then there was only Lake Michigan.

Walker slapped a palm to the three power buttons on the console. The fighter's drive and the throb in Walker's teeth died. With both hands on the altitude control, he hauled back.

The compact alien ship hit the water's surface like a flat stone, skipping. Once, twice, three times, the craft bounced off the water and slammed into it again. Then the bone-jarring ride halted. The fighter rested, floating on the surface of Lake Michigan.

"That was one hell of a landing, Sam!" Paul's shaky voice came from the tail of the ship. "If you were trying to impress me, you succeeded. Next time, I'd be just as impressed if you could just— Sam, we're taking water!"

The crackling sputter of shorting electrical circuitry jerked Walker's head around. Sparks erupted from a nasty-looking split in the fighter's right side through which gushed a fountain of water.

"Out!" Walker depressed the red button at the upper left-hand corner of the console. "Get out before it takes us down with it."

Paul didn't question the order. Tugging off his boots while he scrambled forward, he dived through the opening door and into the lake perhaps three seconds before Walker hurled himself out the half-opened door. Neither looked back at the sinking fighter, but swam for Chicago's skyline a mile to the west.

They had covered a quarter of a mile when the rumble of an inboard motor drew their attention to the southwest. A Coast Guard launch approached. Five minutes later they were pulled from the drink, wrapped in blankets, and handed cups of hot coffee.

"A radio?" Paul asked. "Do you have a radio aboard? I have to contact the police."

Walker smiled, remembering Officer Jim and the official greeting he had received on his first return from Alicia's Mother Ship. The young Coast Guard lieutenant in command didn't question Paul Nordine even though he was dressed in the reds of a Visitor shock trooper. The officer simply escorted the well-known resistance leader to a small cabin forward.

A few minutes later, Paul returned to the coffee he had left with Walker. He took a long sip and said, "I've arranged for Steve to be picked up."

Two police squad cars met the Coast Guard launch at Chicago's Yacht Basin. With a round of handshaking and heartfelt thank you's to the crew for saving them from the long swim to shore and for the dry clothing they now wore, Paul and Walker rushed to the squad cars.

"Four other squads are positioned around the Art Institute," a Captain Beeman informed them as they slid into the back seat of the lead car. "The chief said you were to call the shots on this one."

"Good." Paul nodded while Beeman eased the car onto the northbound lane of Lake Shore Drive. "Steve isn't responsible for what he did. The Visitors converted him—no man can resist that damned conversion chamber. Believe me, he isn't responsible, just another victim."

Beeman might not have understood, but Walker did. The nothingness Alicia had introduced him to within the conversion chamber was still very real in his mind. He could only guess at what private horrors the Mother Ship's commander had unlocked in Steve Tyford's brain to twist and warp him until she had remolded him into an unquestioning slave.

The drive to the Institute took less than five minutes. Beeman pulled into the parking lot, halted, and glanced to the back seat. Paul's gaze was on the building ahead. His expression was that of a man considering all his options.

When he looked at the police captain, he said, "Give us time to get inside, then have your men surround the building. If we're not out with Steve in ten minutes, come in and do whatever is necessary. Just keep in mind that he's not responsible for anything he does."

Beeman nodded in agreement. Paul opened the car door and stepped out. Walker followed him from the parking lot into the Institute.

"With luck, we can pull this off quietly without anyone getting hurt." Paul paused a few feet from Steve's office. He drew a deep breath, then opened the door.

Tyford sat behind a bare desk talking with two men standing before him. His eyes went wide as he saw Paul.

"You? How?"

In the next instant, all hell broke loose. Tyford leaped from his seat while simultaneously the two men in front of the desk pivoted and launched themselves at the door. A human locomotive slammed into Walker's chest, hurling him across the hall. He felt his back, then his head hit the opposite wall. Then the world went black.

When he awoke, it was with a throbbing headache and a knot the size of a goose egg on the back of his skull. He lay on an office sofa with a paramedic standing over him. At the young man's insistence, he spoke his name. Walker then told the man how many fingers the other was rudely jabbing in his face and where he could shove them.

Paul Nordine chuckled behind the paramedic. "I think he's sufficiently recovered."

"I advise that he be taken to a hospital for X-rays, just to be on the safe side," the paramedic said while he closed a large metal container that looked like a tool box. "You can never be too safe with head injuries."

The young man walked from the office and left Paul staring down at Walker. "You want a ride to the hospital?"

Walker shook his head and immediately regretted it when the throbbing increased twofold. "What happened to Steve?"

"Beeman and his men captured him and the two others as they were getting into a car in the parking lot," Paul answered.

"Two others?" Walker groaned. He had forgotten about the gorillas who had thrown him into the wall.

"They were two more of Alicia's converts within the resistance, best as I could piece together," Paul continued. "The police have all three safely locked away in a hospital psychiatric ward."

"Psychiatric ward?" Walker sat up and waited until the world quit spinning before he glanced up at Paul.

"The doctors say that one day, with luck and a lot of work, they might be able to untangle the mess Alicia made of their minds," Paul said. "Until that day it's best to keep them under observation where they can't hurt themselves or anyone else."

Walker sucked at his teeth. *Victims. First Kathleen, Jennifer, and Janus. Now Steve Tyford and the other two men. Six more victims of the Visitors' reign.*

"Certain you don't want someone to take you to a hospital for X-rays?" Paul asked.

Walker caught himself before he shook his head; he simply said, "No."

"Good, because I've got a meeting with the Mayor and the chief of police in fifteen minutes," Paul said. "We've still got Gerald's Arlington Park outpost to deal with. I thought you might like to go along."

Walker pushed to his feet, ignored the momentary spin of the room, and grinned. "If you're waiting for me, you're wasting time."

Chapter Seventeen

Walker peered south from the doorway of the deserted supermarket in which Janus had first given Kathleen and him the news of the Visitors' defeat. Even with binoculars he saw no sign of shock trooper activity among the deserted barns.

"Think they've pulled out?" Paul questioned in a whisper. "It looks awfully quiet over there."

"The planes saw no signs of shuttles all day." Walker reminded him of the police reconnaissance planes that had flown a wide circle about the abandoned racetrack while the resistance forces took their positions around Arlington Park. "Even this far from the city, I don't think Alicia and Gerald would risk an evacuation in daylight."

Walker paused and gave the stable area another cursory perusal. "No, the Visitors are still in there, hiding in the stalls. In another half hour, when it's dark, they'll come slithering out of their holes."

Paul's gaze dipped to his wristwatch. "Another thirty minutes." He lifted his binoculars and stared back at the racetrack.

Thirty minutes. Walker grimaced. In a half hour the rabbit would finally face the lizards. This time there would be no scurrying for cover, no popping into a burrow to cower.

Leaning against the wall next to the door, he studied the fifty men and women who squatted along a wide aisle leading to the back of the store. Each clutched a rifle in his or her hands. Here and there a bayonet or a hand grenade dangled from a belt—the rewards of a National Guard armory raid during the months Paul and his organization had waged their underground war against the Visitors.

There were no professionals here. Chicago's police had their hands full keeping their postwar city from exploding. In spite of the increased food and medical supplies, there were still shortages. Riots were a common daily and nightly occurrence. Except for three helicopters which would be sent in as air support five minutes after the attack began, the police had left Gerald and his force to Paul Nordine.

The black-clad warriors crouched here were ordinary people who refused to see their planet sucked dry by alien invaders. Without question they had answered Paul's call to arms. They came to fight an enemy that they had been reassured had been driven from the face of their world forever.

"There, crossing between the barns to the left." Paul elbowed Walker and handed him the binoculars. "A guard. You were right. They're patrolling the track's perimeters."

Walker barely glimpsed the red flash of a shock trooper's uniform as a lone soldier hastened from one barn to another. He got a better look when the Visitor walked out the opposite side of the stable and crossed to the next. Walker handed the binoculars back to Paul.

The guards were the reason they waited for the night. Darkness increased their chances of success. Black-clad and with faces blackened with greasepaint, they would be shadows in the night as they moved toward the chain-link fence enclosing Arlington Park.

"Fifteen minutes," Paul whispered when he checked his watch again.

And when we reach the fence? Walker's grip tightened around the deer rifle he carried.

Paul's plan was simple, perhaps even primitive. Four strike teams, each fifty strong, waited on each side of the track. At nine o'clock, when the sun's last glow had faded from the sky, they would move out, encircling their target. At 9:15 they'd hit the fence with the hand grenades, ripping holes in the barrier that separated them from the Visitor outpost.

Once inside the track, the four teams would fight their way inward, converging on the parking lot that lay between the stable area and the main racecourse. In their wake, they would leave fire—if necessary. Should Gerald's troopers decide to barricade themselves in one of the track's structures, Paul had decided against a long, drawn-out battle. His orders were, "Burn them out."

Simple and crude, Walker thought, but effective. Resistance headquarters at Lake Zurich had contained only two hundred antitoxin tablets. That meant Gerald's force could be no larger than two hundred—fewer, counting those Janus, Jennifer, and he had killed. Paul wanted them all, dead or alive. In one quick, hard-hitting strike he intended to eliminate the possibility of toxin-immune Visitors ever returning to his city or the world.

A nagging, achy throb pulsed at the roots of Walker's molars. He stiffened. "Paul there's . . ."

"Shuttles!" Paul spoke through clenched teeth. "Five of them coming in out of the west! Something's going on in there."

Walker looked out the door. The insectal white forms of the squad vehicles were like pale wisps, phantom things as they slipped noiselessly through the air in a tight delta formation. Together they hovered over the center of the racetrack, then disappeared when they descended behind the barns.

The myriad questions filling Walker's head were never vocalized. He wasn't given the chance to ask them.

Paul glanced at his watch and looked up at Walker. "Nine o'clock. Let's move out!"

Turning to the waiting men and women, Paul lifted an arm and waved them forward. Silently they stood, rifles ready, and hastened forward. Every other member of the strike team held a gasoline can, the type usually carried in trucks or cars for an emergency.

Outside, the black-clad resistance fighters split in two files, one running east and the other west across the empty parking lot toward Northwest Highway where they spread out along the road's shoulder. Paul's arm rose and fell again. Fifty inky forms moved across the band of concrete to drop beside the railroad track that ran along the north side of the racetrack.

Paul tugged back the sleeve of the black sweat shirt he wore. Face pressed close to his watch, he waited. When he rolled to his back, it wasn't for another hand signal. He slipped a grenade from his belt, pulled the pin, flipped the clip, whisper-counted three seconds aloud, then lobbed the explosive in a high arc toward the fence.

Seconds that seemed to drag to hours passed before the thunderous roar rent the evening air. Then there was nothing but explosions! From around the racetrack the Chicagoans blasted their way through the only obstacle between them and the army of shock troopers.

There was no more waiting. Battle cry tearing from his throat, Walker leaped to his feet and ran forward. To each side of him the fifty men of Paul's strike team pushed across the railroad track toward the jagged rents in the fence. Their voices rose, melting with those of the other teams until a blood-chilling yowl filled the night.

Paul ducked through the hole he had made in the chain-link barrier first. Walker ran at his heels. The now familiar blue-white bursts of pulse-beam energy came from the right. A woman screamed. A shadow-dark form jerked rigid and tumbled facedown to the ground.

Walker swung around. His rifle jerked up, its barrel homing in on the burst-illuminated form half hidden in the shedrow of a barn. Walker's finger squeezed the trigger twice. The deer rifle barked.

Two armor-piercing bullets struck their target. The energy rifle was silenced as the shock trooper behind it flew backward under the impact. He slammed into the door of a stall, slid to the ground, and crumpled there in an unmoving heap.

Beside him, Paul's rifle spoke. A red-uniformed Visitor stepped from the shadows and dropped before he could lift his weapon and fire.

"Where the hell are they?" Paul glanced over a shoulder at Walker. "I thought they would be all over us the minute we tried for the fence!"

Walker frowned. He had been so busy with the two shock troopers, he hadn't noticed that they were met by only token resistance. The sporadic gunshots that echoed over the racetrack told the same tale. The strike teams only faced the guards placed about the track's perimeter. Where was Gerald's army?

A dark, writhing thought wiggled from the back of Walker's mind. His stomach did a sickening lurch.

"The shuttles, Paul!" Walker pushed ahead of the Chicago resistance leader. He started to trot, then ran south toward the parking lot where the Visitor craft had landed. "Gerald's evacuating his troops! He's trying to get away!"

In long, ground-covering strides Walker moved to the

barn on his left. And nearly ran into Janus's old Pinto which the Visitors had hidden there. Dodging the battered car, he sprinted to the end of the shedrow and ran to the opposite side of the barn. A low curse rumbled from his throat when his eyes confirmed his fears.

A hundred yards to the southeast, an asphalt road separating the rows of barns ran into the parking lot. There a line of shock troopers scrambled into the open doors of a shuttle. The barns to the south blocked his view of the rest of the parking lot, but he knew the other four shuttles were there with Gerald's forces piling through their open hatches.

Paul halted beside Walker. His eyes widened when he saw the parking lot scene. "We've got to stop them!"

Paul turned, shouting to the resistance fighters behind him. His orders were simple—forget burning the barns and converge on the parking lot. Walker heard the order being passed between the men and women. In a minute or less the four strike teams would rush the parking lot.

A minute might be too late! Walker's gaze narrowed. He had dealt with Gerald's shuttles once before. Janus had unknowingly given him the method to do so again.

The hollow clank of a dropped gasoline can spun Walker around. Behind him a black-clad resistance fighter tossed away the burden that weighed him down. To the right another discarded gas can hit the ground. Walker knew what he had to do.

"Sam? Where are you going?" Paul called when Walker ran back down the shedrow.

Walker gave no answer to what must have appeared to be a cowardly retreat. Slinging his rifle over a shoulder, he scooped the first gas can from the ground, then the second. An instant later he was beside Janus's old car. The keys were still in the ignition.

Placing the discarded gasoline containers in the back seat, Walker slid behind the steering wheel. He pumped the accelerator twice and twisted the key. The engine coughed, caught, then purred in a smooth mechanical hum.

Walker rammed the four-speed stick shift into first and eased off the clutch. The Pinto edged down the shedrow. A sharp twist of the steering wheel when he reached the tackrooms at the end of the barn, and he swung from beneath the shedrow. He spun the wheel again and did a 300-degree-plus turn onto the asphalt road.

Hell reigned in the parking lot. No longer did the shock troopers leisurely march into the shuttle. With rifles turned on the attacking resistance fighters, they encircled the craft, protecting it with a steady barrage of blue energy bursts. Here and there Walker saw the helmeted alien warriors double over and drop to the concrete as the hail of lead Paul's team pumped into the Visitors claimed more victims.

Death was not one-sided. Again and again, the sizzling bolts found their marks. Night-camouflaged men and women fell, their lives given freely to the world they fought to defend.

Knuckles white from the pressure with which he gripped the steering wheel, Walker drew a deep breath and clenched his teeth. His right hand reached down and wrapped around the gear-shift knob. His right foot pressed the accelerator to the floor.

Rubber screamed against asphalt as the battered Pinto responded and lurched forward. Walker shifted into second gear, then third.

Fifty feet from the ring of shock troopers surrounding the shuttle, Walker switched on the headlights and toed them to bright. He saw the barrels of the Visitors' weapons swing about to face a new human offensive.

He didn't wait for the blasts he knew would come. Shoving open the door, he threw himself from the car. He hit the asphalt and—

Blackness rushed over him in a tidal wave, following the

sharp, painful crack that resounded through his head when he struck the pavement.

No! He struggled against the darkness, refusing to let it swallow him, suck him down into oblivion. Somewhere he heard screams, the roar of an explosion. He tried to open his eyes, to see if his car-turned-unguided-missile had struck its target. The blackness weighted his eyes, pulled him downward.

Plop-a-plop-a-plop-a-plop-a.

A steady mechanical rhythm wedged into the darkness. He reached out, grasping it, hauling himself up.

Helicopters! His eyes blinked open. The three police helicopters hovered high above the parking lot. Their searchlights played across the concrete, illuminating the Visitors below for the marksmen riding inside the aircraft.

Walker pushed to an elbow, ignoring the awful throbbing in his head. The blazing light of one burning Pinto and one shuttle aided the airborne sharpshooters in their task.

With a humorless smile on his lips, Walker rose, found his rifle, and staggered toward the barn fronting the parking lot. By the time he reached the shedrow, he had regained a semblance of control over his arms and legs, enough to edge around the barn and open a stall door. Once inside, he used the stall's wall for cover while he emptied his rifle into the circles of Visitors that ringed the four remaining shuttles.

Dropping to a knee, Walker fumbled with his pockets and withdrew a fistful of cartridges which he stuffed into the empty rifle. When he raised the rifle again, his attention focused on a familiar form, a blonde-haired man whose human-disguised eyes lay hidden behind dark sunglasses.

Gerald! Walker carefully sighted down the barrel of the deer rifle. His finger curled around the trigger.

In the next instant, the sky exploded.

Energy bolts turned skyward had found a target. Like a

spinning dragonfly cloaked in flame, one of the police helicopters plummeted down. Human screams railed through the night, then abruptly died when the rotary craft slammed into the ground.

Walker's gaze shot back to Gerald. He was gone, had disappeared in the chaotic scramble of shock troopers who tried to fight their way onto four remaining shuttles. Cursing, Walker began to squeeze his trigger again, firing at the nearest of the shuttles.

Five shots barked from his rifle when he jerked back and pressed against the stall's wall. Blue bolts strafed down the shedrow, two finding their way through the open door and flaming out harmlessly against the rear wall of the stall.

When the sizzle of deadly energy died, he swung back and lifted his rifle. His finger paused. One of the shuttles closed its doors. Silently it rose into the air.

Simultaneously the two remaining helicopters descended toward the escaping squad vehicle. Walker stared on in horror. The two chopper pilots never saw each other's craft. Metal screamed in agony as the two helicopters collided in midair. Fire, glass, and the twisted remains of the two choppers rained down.

The still-spinning rotor of one of the helicopters sliced into the side of the rising shuttle. A heartbeat later it exploded.

The burning carcasses of three ships, one alien and two human, crashed into the parking lot. Like a river of flame, fire swept across the field of concrete and engulfed the three remaining shuttles. In a moment they exploded in balls of flame.

The inferno devoured anything in its path. Shock troopers abandoned their rifles, perferring to fight the flames licking at their uniforms than the human fighters who surrounded them. Screams, inhuman hissing screams, rose to mingle with the angry roar of the fire.

Walker lowered his rifle and closed his eyes. Fire was an ugly, dirty death, even for hated enemies.

The smell of aviation fuel and charred reptilian bodies hung thick and oily in the air. Walker turned from the scorched parking lot. With a shake of his head, he walked, not caring where his strides took him. He needed fresh air, needed to escape the vision of burning, screaming Visitors etched in his mind.

None of those in the parking lot had escaped. All had been consumed by the fire. Walker drew a heavy breath. The hellish scene would never be far from his thoughts, always waiting to haunt him.

Behind him, he heard the voices of Paul's strike teams as they counted off. The tally of this small battle still wasn't in. The number of the dead resistance fighters remained to be added to the two hundred shock troopers who had died in the attack. He didn't want to hear the final count, didn't want to add that burden to his already weary mind.

Even the fact that they had stopped—totally destroyed—Gerald and his toxin-immune soldiers provided little comfort. He was too close to those burning shock troopers. Their dying screams still echoed in his brain.

The creak of a rusty hinge drew Walker's gaze to the left as he walked to the opposite side of the barn. The bottom portion of a stall door opened. A man in a red uniform edged out and stood.

No . . . no. Walker attempted to deny what his eyes saw—the blonde hair—the dark glasses. The Visitor high captain had somehow escaped the parking lot, had hidden while his troops died.

"Gerald!" Walker heard himself say.

Gerald spun around, his right hand closing about the holstered energy pistol on his hip. Walker's right hand jerked up, lifting the muzzle of his deer rifle. He squeezed the trigger.

A fraction of a second after the resounding bark of his shot, Gerald yowled. The pistol flew from his hand and lost itself in the darkness.

The Visitor didn't stand there clutching his wounded hand. Gerald hissed and charged!

Walker's finger tightened about the trigger and squeezed. The rifle responded with a sharp click—it was empty.

It was a fact Walker barely grasped before the alien slammed into him. The useless rifle flew from his hand as he tumbled, falling to the sandy shedrow.

"You!" Gerald's voice reverberated as he hissed down at Walker. "At least I shall have the pleasure of killing you— to repay in part all that you've cost me!"

Walker couldn't dodge the arm that shot out. Nor could he escape the hand that clenched the front of his shirt and effortlessly wrenched him into the air. The best he could manage was to awkwardly swing a fist.

Gerald roared. Walker saw the flick of a forked tongue behind human lips, saw the green and black mottled scales beneath the Visitor's torn human mask. Then Walker sailed through the air, tossed aside like a child's doll.

He hit the ground hard. Air rushed from his lungs, leaving him gasping. He shook his head in an attempt to clear his vision. And he saw Gerald ripping away his human disguise. The face and head revealed were right out of a nightmare.

A lipless mouth opened to reveal two rows of razorlike teeth and an angry, flicking red forked tongue. Snake or lizard did not describe Gerald's reptilian countenance. Those were words for earthly reptiles. The hissing creature that stalked forward was totally alien, a life form from another world.

Walker had seen the glaring, slitted yellow-orange eyes

before. Once. Those eyes had stared at him from the head of
a Florida alligator.

Walker's arms flew out on each side of him, trying to find
leverage in the sandy ground to push to his feet, to scramble
away from the reptilian-headed death that came to claim his
life. His right hand touched something cold and metallic.

My rifle! He recognized the barrel, closed his hand
around tempered steel. As Gerald stooped to reach for him,
Walker swung the rifle.

Solidly the rifle butt smacked into Gerald's temple. He
roared. Human-disguised hands clutched the side of his
head. He stumbled back.

Walker scrambled to his feet, flipped the rifle around, and
attacked, using the barrel like an iron pipe. Again and again
he brought the weapon down on Gerald's green-scaled head.
He saw the leathery flesh part and green blood ooze from
the open wound. Still he pounded, driving the Visitor to his
knees, stopping only when Gerald fell facedown in the
sand.

For minutes Walker stood over the motionless body, chest
heaving and eyes searching for the smallest twitch from the
dead Visitor. When he heard Paul call to him, he looked up.
The resistance leader and six others in his command stood at
the end of the shedrow.

"It's over, Sam," Paul said gently. "You've won. He's
dead. You can toss away the rifle now."

"Over.' Walker nodded, glancing down at his rifle and
the green blood dripping from the barrel. With a curse, he
threw the weapon into the night. "Over for now."

Walker pushed his way past Paul and those behind him.
He needed fresh air more than ever.

Chapter Eighteen

"Fire sweeping toward my position. Evacuation shuttles three and four are engulfed in flames. Will attempt to lift before . . ."

Static crackled from the speaker in the control room of the Chicago Mother Ship. Alicia's aquamarine eyes shifted to the communications officer. The black-tressed woman who had monitored the communications from the Arlington Park outpost shook her head.

"Sensor readings?" Alicia glanced at an officer with short-cropped hair across the control room.

"Readings negative," the man replied. "All the shuttles have been destroyed."

A cold finger tapped at the base of Alicia's spine. A numbing chill ran up her back. *No! It can't be! It can't end like this!*

She closed her eyes. The silence filling the control room pressed down on her. She had held the key to Earth in her hand. How had it slipped away? What had gone wrong?

"Commander Alicia," Lewis's voice broke the silence,

"faced with this failure, we feel that your immediate resignation is required."

"Resignation?" Alicia could not restrain her anger. Her eyes flew open and she stared at the instrument consoles, her back to the five who stood in judgment of her actions. "Lewis, you are a pompous ass! This is *my* ship! You are but a guest here at my pleasure. While you and your cronies sat on your fat backsides, cringing and sweating, I—only I—took action. Do not presume to tell me what course I should take now."

Alicia spun about. The hate-filled glare of her eyes faded to a bewildered confusion. Ian stood, his pistol drawn and aimed directly at her chest. "What is this?" she demanded.

"Your end," the London Mother Ship commander answered coolly. "The opportunity to resign was Lewis's idea, a matter of protocol he felt should be observed. We've observed it. Now we are removing you from command. You alone authorized the Chicago conversion. You alone shall face Our Great Leader's wrath for its failure. Until our return to our home world, you will be held in isolation to make sure others are not contaminated by your philosophies. Guards, take her!"

The shock trooper guards—her guards—within the control room didn't hesitate. Six of them surrounded her, two taking her arms.

"You swine! You can't do this!" Alicia screamed. "This is my ship! *My ship!*"

"*Was* your ship. A replacement will be easy to find. An officer with less of an appetite for personal glory." Ian waved the guards and their prisoner from the control room.

None of the five Mother Ship commanders gave Alicia so much as a second glance when she was dragged screaming from their presence.

*   *   *

Walker stood beside a small mound in Arlington Park's center field. The tulips on Kathleen's grave had died, but already the buds of other flowers prepared to open. Walker silently nodded his approval.

"Sam," Paul Nordine called to him.

Walker looked up and watched the resistance leader walk toward him. The man ran a hand through his thick black hair and glanced at the grandstand when he reached Walker's side.

"They found Janus's body," Paul said. "My men are removing it right now. He'll receive a proper burial."

"He wanted a marble stone with words," Walker said, remembering the comments Janus had made the day they had buried Kathleen. "He wanted those who came after him to know he had lived."

"I'll see that he gets that," Paul answered. He turned to the east. "It'll be daylight soon."

Walker glanced at the horizon. The coming dawn edged back the last purples and grays of the night.

"It will be a good day, Sam. A clean day. Last night we removed a cancer that would have destroyed our city—our world," Paul said. "Chicago is safe."

"For now." Walker shivered as he recalled Jennifer's comments on the shuttle. "They'll be back, Paul. Earth is too big a prize for them to ignore. Someday, somehow they'll find a way to come back. There's so much we don't know about them, about what their science is capable of creating. They have ships that can span the stars. We've all but abandoned our space program. There's so much we don't know."

"There's a lot we don't know." Paul agreed. "But we do know that the Visitors are still out there. While they're out there, the possibility they'll return will always hang over our heads. For now, all we can do is watch the skies and be prepared to face the ships that will come one day."

Paul paused for a breath and looked at Walker. "We have to build again, Sam. We have to be ready for the Visitors' return."

"Freedom is something a man must fight for every day." Walker repeated the words Janus had once spoken to him.

"Day and night," Paul said. "It's a job that will take every man and woman and child we can get. You once refused to join us. Will you reconsider now?"

Walker looked down at Kathleen's grave, then glanced back at Paul. "What do you have in mind?"

"More hard work than one man should even think about." Paul grinned. He extended a hand to Walker.

"We're not getting it done here." Walker took the man's hand and shook it. "Shouldn't we be heading back to Chicago? I think you mentioned something about rebuilding a city."

Watch for

THE FLORIDA PROJECT

next in the V series
from
Pinnacle Books

coming in February!